DISPLACED

ALSO BY DEAN HUGHES

FOUR-FOUR-TWO
MISSING IN ACTION
SEARCH AND DESTROY
SOLDIER BOYS

DISPLACED
DEAN HUGHES

Atheneum
NEW YORK LONDON TORONTO
SYDNEY NEW DELHI

FOR MY GREAT-GRANDSON,
BENJAMIN HSIUNG RUSSELL

atheneum

An imprint of Simon & Schuster Children's Publishing Division • 1230 Avenue
of the Americas, New York, New York 10020 • This book is a work of fiction. Any
references to historical events, real people, or real places are used fictitiously. Other
names, characters, places, and events are products of the author's imagination, and
any resemblance to actual events or places or persons, living or dead, is entirely
coincidental. • Text copyright © 2020 by Dean Hughes • Jacket illustration copyright
© 2020 by Darren Hopes • All rights reserved, including the right of reproduction in
whole or in part in any form. • Atheneum logo is a trademark of Simon & Schuster, Inc. •
For information about special discounts for bulk purchases, please contact Simon &
Schuster Special Sales at 1-866-506-1949 or business@simonandschuster.com. • The
Simon & Schuster Speakers Bureau can bring authors to your live event. For more
information or to book an event, contact the Simon & Schuster Speakers Bureau at
1-866-248-3049 or visit our website at www.simonspeakers.com. • The text for this
book was set in Chronicle Text G1. • Manufactured in the United States of America •
First Edition • 10 9 8 7 6 5 4 3 2 1 • Library of Congress Cataloging-in-
Publication Data • Names: Hughes, Dean, 1943– author. • Title: Displaced / Dean
Hughes. • Description: First edition. | New York : Atheneum, [2020] | Audience: Ages
12 Up. | Audience: Grades 7–9. | Summary: Toma and Malek, two thirteen-year-old
Syrian children living in Beirut, struggle to provide for their families in a country
that can be hostile against refugees like them, but they maintain hope that there is
a way out of their seemingly impossible situation. • Identifiers: LCCN 2020012974 |
ISBN 9781534452329 (hardcover) | ISBN 9781534452343 (eBook) • Subjects:
CYAC: Refugees—Fiction. | Syrians—Lebanon—Fiction. | Lebanon—Fiction. |
Friendship—Fiction. | Survival—Fiction. | Belonging (Social psychology)—Fiction. •
Classification: LCC PZ7.H87312 Di 2020 | DDC [Fic]—dc23 • LC record available at
https://lccn.loc.gov/2020012974

THIS MOMENT DOES NOT DEFINE THEM
[THE ESTIMATED SIXTY MILLION REFUGEES
IN THE WORLD], BUT OUR RESPONSE
WILL HELP DEFINE US.

—PATRICK KEARON

1

Hadi Saleh was sitting on a stack of concrete blocks. He was leaning forward, looking down, the hood of his jacket pulled over his head. He could feel drops of rain pat against his shoulders and he could see the splashes on the wet sidewalk near his feet. The wheels of cars rolled slowly past him, sloshing out little currents of water against the curb. He crossed his arms against his chest to stay as warm as he could, and he waited. He knew, without thinking about it, how long it took until the light changed and the cars stopped, knew he had only a few more seconds to himself before he would have to face the drivers again. Still, he waited. A few drivers always ran the red light, and then the intermittent blast of car horns would turn into a full, wild blare.

It was always the same: honking, yelling, and frantic drivers maneuvering through the nightmare traffic, stopping only when they had no other choice. But finally the wheels did stop rolling, and Hadi got up. He walked around to the driver's side of the first car in line. He pulled cardboard packages of gum from his jacket pocket—Chiclets in four flavors: cinnamon, spearmint, fruit, and peppermint. He fanned out the boxes on his palms close to the window so the driver could see the choices. But the woman inside didn't look at him; she stared straight ahead. It was the usual thing.

So Hadi walked over to the first car in the inside lane, and he held the gum out again, this time on the passenger side. This driver, a young man, glanced at him, then shook his head. Hadi didn't say anything, didn't plead. He had tried that in the beginning, long ago, and found it was a waste of his time. He walked to the next car, and the next, back and forth between the two lanes.

An older man with a stubbly beard and tired eyes glanced toward him from one of the cars. His window was halfway open, even in the rain. He was smoking, holding his cigarette close to the window so the breeze drew the smoke up and out of the car. When Hadi stopped and presented his packages of gum, the man said without looking at Hadi, in a low, hostile voice, "Why do you do this every day? No one wants your gum." Hadi turned to walk away, but he heard the man say, "You Syrian pigs need to get out of our country. All of you."

Hadi didn't respond, didn't even give the man's words a second thought. He heard such things every day. Words didn't change what he had to do.

The clock in his head was telling him that the stoplight

would soon turn green and the cars would start to move. Already, drivers who were nine and ten back from the intersection were beginning to honk. He had no idea why they thought that would speed things up. He made one last offer, got another headshake, then cut between two cars to the sidewalk and walked down the little slope to the corner, back to his stack of concrete blocks.

Hadi sat down and leaned forward. He listened to the patting of the rain on his hood again. At least the storm was light today. Rain came often to Beirut in the winter, sometimes falling in torrents. And even when it didn't rain, days were cold, sometimes windy. He was wearing a sweatshirt under his rain jacket—one that had been given to him by a charity organization in his neighborhood—but his feet were freezing, his hands, his face. Still, he was relieved there was no flooding at the bottom of the hill today. The splashes from the cars weren't reaching him.

Before long he heard the slowing of tires, and the crazy honking started again. Hadi looked up, waited a few more seconds. There was a cabstand to the south, directly across the street. Cabbies sat there and smoked and talked. Most of them were Lebanese, not Syrians, and they liked to give Hadi a hard time—mostly just teasing, but sometimes in filthy language. Hadi didn't like them very much, but one of them, a man named Rashid, let him store his chewing gum in a locked cabinet in the cabstand. Hadi got along all right with Rashid, but he tried to avoid the other men.

Hadi got up, started again. He walked to each car. The drivers stared away from him, or they shook their heads. This time no one cursed him or insulted him. But that didn't matter to Hadi. What mattered was that he sold no gum again.

Almost an hour went by before a woman, with her window already down, smiled and handed Hadi one thousand Lebanese pounds—the smallest bill the government printed. The woman chose the red box—cinnamon—and she said in Arabic, "Thank you, *habibi*. I hope you're not too cold."

The woman was pretty, and she was still smiling. She had called him "my love."

"*Allah yehmik,*" he said. "God protect you."

She nodded, and he thanked her. *"Chokran."* He walked away, and he felt better. He finally had some money—a thousand pounds, or lira, as they were also called. He needed ten or twelve thousand to have a decent day—fifteen or twenty thousand for a great day. But it had taken a long time to get this first sale. Rainy days were bad. Car windows were mostly rolled up, traffic was congested, and people were unhappy, even more than usual.

But the woman had been nice to him. That was something.

The next hour was a little better. He received a five-hundred-pound coin from an older man who simply gave it to him without taking the gum, and a young man gave him two one-thousand-pound bills. Not often did anyone give him so much. But another man hissed at him, "I can smell you from here. You should stay in the sewer, where you belong."

The rain let up after a time, but Hadi still looked at the sidewalk, not at the cars, and he listened for them to stop. Maybe, with the sun peeking out, people would be happier. Maybe more of them would buy from him. But there was no telling. Some days were better than others. "*Inshallah,*" his father always said. "God willing." But his father was never happy when Hadi came to him at the end of a day with only five or six thousand pounds—God willing or not. That much would buy a package of flat bread and a little rice, but it would leave nothing for other expenses. Hadi and his father had to earn enough each day to buy food for nine in the Saleh family, but they also had to save each day to pay for rent and electricity. The rent for their single room, for a month, was 240,000 Lebanese pounds, and there was nothing cheaper anywhere in Beirut.

Hadi wished that he could sleep for a little while. His brain felt numb—dulled by the daily buzz of tires on pavement, deadened to the curses he heard. Every day he saw Lebanese children walking by on their way to school. They laughed and made jokes with each other. He sometimes wondered what that would be like, to sit in school—not out in the rain—and read books, learn things. But it didn't help to wonder; he was better off letting his mind drift, not thinking too much.

But then he spotted a car he knew. It was the couple he called "the foreigners" because they didn't speak much Arabic. They always gave him money, and they didn't take any gum. So he stood, waited, and when the light changed, walked directly to their car. It was what he needed today: to hear them greet him with the clumsy Arabic they knew and to see their happiness. Today they handed him not only a thousand pounds but a shawarma sandwich. They gave him something to eat fairly often, once a week or so.

The foreign man always dressed neatly, looked like a teacher, a grandfather. He was a small man with a gentle voice. His wife was more lively. She would lean toward the driver's-side window and tell him, "Nice to see you, Hadi." She had white hair, but she didn't seem old. Her voice was strong. He remembered a grandmother like that, his mother's mother, back in Syria. She had lived in a village in the mountains, and when his family had visited, she had always fed them lots of good food. She baked the best sweets he had ever tasted. He sometimes wondered whether he would see her again. Mama said she was getting old.

"Too bad for rain," the foreign woman said.

"Yes," Hadi told her. "But a little water won't melt me."

It was what Baba often said, but Hadi could see that the woman didn't understand. Still, she smiled and said, "We see you tomorrow."

"Yes. Thank you for the shawarma. *Allah yebarkek.* May

God prosper you." He didn't smile very often, but he smiled now as he listened to the man say something that didn't sound Arabic but sounded friendly. Hadi waved to them as they drove away, and then he walked back to his seat by the corner. He ate a few bites of the shawarma, savoring it slowly. He would only eat half and take the rest home. If he didn't earn much today, he could share his sandwich with his younger brother Khaled, who was always hungry and didn't seem to be growing the way he should.

The clouds gradually broke up and the sun shone brightly at times. Most people were still turning him down, but the clearing weather and those few bites of the sandwich made everything seem a little better.

Early in the afternoon Hadi saw a boy standing on a corner on the west side of the five-way intersection. He watched as the boy crossed the street. He was taller than Hadi, and older. His hair was slick and black, but the tone of his skin was lighter than Hadi's. He was carrying a big plastic bundle. It was the kind that Hadi had seen filled with packages of tissues.

But now the cars in front of Hadi had stopped. So he made his usual walk up the slight hill, back and forth between lanes, once again offering his gum at each car window. No one wanted any, and no one said much to him, so Hadi crossed to the sidewalk and started back to his spot. But now the tall boy was standing at the corner, waiting. Hadi didn't like the look of this.

As Hadi approached, the boy smiled. "*Marhaba*," he said. "My name's Malek."

Hadi didn't respond. He didn't know what the boy wanted.

"Kamal told me I should work on this corner."

"This is my corner," Hadi said.

"From now on it's mine," Malek said, still smiling. "Maybe Kamal will give you a different one."

"I don't know who Kamal is, and I'm not leaving my corner." Hadi and his father had taken a bus to this side of Beirut almost two years back, and they had decided together that this was a good intersection for Hadi to work. Once in a while another boy or girl had shown up and worked on one of the other corners in the intersection, but no one had stayed long, and no one had ever questioned Hadi's right to his place.

Malek's smile faded. He looked confused. "I thought Kamal assigned all the corners," he said.

Hadi thought he knew what was going on. There were gangs in Lebanon that moved in on neighborhoods and took control. They claimed ownership of the streets, and they placed boys and girls—now mostly Syrian refugees, though it hadn't always been that way—on the corners to beg for money or to sell things, and they took much of the money the kids earned. Hadi and his father had learned about this when they had first arrived in Beirut, but most of the gangs operated in Hamra and other expensive areas. It was why

Baba had chosen Bauchrieh, on the northeast side of the city. No gangs had bothered them there.

Hadi looked Malek straight on. "I'm telling you, this is my corner. I'm not leaving."

Malek nodded, and for no reason that Hadi understood, he smiled again. "I'll tell you what," he said. "It looks to me like plenty of cars stop at this light. I'll take one lane and you take the other. If we get to the last cars in line, we can cross over. You have gum and I have tissues. So we won't be a bother to each other."

"I know lots of the drivers here," Hadi said. "They know me. It's my corner."

"I understand. But if I leave, I'll have to tell Kamal that you stopped me from working. I know for sure he won't like that."

Hadi knew what Malek was talking about. He had heard about beatings—even a street boy that someone had found in a garbage dumpster, dead. But Hadi also had his family to think of. It was all he could do to make enough money to buy a little food for them. He couldn't take a chance on some of *his* money going to this new boy. So he looked hard into Malek's eyes and said, "I work by myself."

"Let's try it my way, and I won't tell Kamal that you stayed. If he finds out, he might make you leave, but if you get rid of me, you'll definitely be in trouble."

Hadi stared at this smiling boy. He didn't seem like the street children he knew. He talked more. He was wearing a jacket that looked new, not faded and worn like the ones the charity houses handed out.

"Have you ever worked on the streets before?" Hadi asked.

"No. Maybe you can teach me some tricks. What works best?"

Hadi shook his head. The guy didn't know anything at all. "There are no tricks," Hadi told him. "You offer the tissues. Some want them. Most don't."

"But I'm good at talking people into things." He laughed. "I'm good-looking, too. All the girls at my school in Syria liked me. I can probably sell a lot of tissues to the women who come by."

This boy was cocky. He had no idea what he was facing. Hadi liked to think what a day on the corner would do to him. Maybe one day would convince him not to come back. But he only told Malek, "No one cares how good-looking you are."

"You sound like you're Syrian too," Malek said. "What city did you come from?"

Hadi didn't want this conversation, but he found himself answering. "Aleppo."

Malek nodded, and he looked almost solemn for the first time. "You got bombed a lot, didn't you?"

"Yes." But Hadi didn't like to think about those days.

"Did you lose your house?"

Hadi nodded, hesitated, but then said, "My house. My school. My whole neighborhood."

"Did your family all get out?"

"Yes. But we lost everything in our apartment. *Everything.*" He thought of the days when his family had had a living room and a television set and Mama had had a kitchen. More than anything, he missed the food his family had eaten back then.

"When did you come to Lebanon?"

"A few years ago. I was eight or nine, I think."

"How long have you been doing this?"

"Since I was eleven. I'm thirteen now."

"I'm fourteen," Malek said. "We came to Beirut last year."

That was more than Hadi needed to know. He wasn't going to be friends with this boy who wanted to take his corner. Still, he found himself asking, "Where from?"

"A village near Damascus."

"Did you get bombed?"

"Yes." He hesitated, and his voice sounded more serious than before. "We had bombs falling all around us. We were scared all the time. We hated to go to bed at night. We were always afraid an attack would come. And then it did. One night our town got blown away. Our family didn't get hurt, but we knew a lot of people who got killed."

Hadi looked into Malek's face and could see that they understood something about each other. He saw the leftover fear in Malek's eyes, knew there was more to him than he had first thought.

They were silent for a few seconds, but then Malek asked, "Which lane of cars do you want?" Hadi thought he knew what Malek was thinking: that they had both said enough about the war. It was better not to think about those days now.

"I'll stay with this outside lane, and you take the middle," Hadi said. "But I'll watch for people I know—who always buy from me—and I'll cross lanes when I see them."

"Sure. Just tell them to buy my tissues too."

Hadi didn't like the idea of doing that. People only had so much to offer, and he couldn't afford for them to give to Malek and not to him. Still, he said, "Okay."

"So, what's your name?" Malek asked as they waited for the cars to slow.

"Hadi."

Malek pulled two packages of tissues from the bundle. "All right, Hadi. *Yallah*," he said. "Let's go." Malek held a package of tissues in each hand, and when the cars stopped, he strode to the middle lane. Hadi heard him talking through the closed window, telling a man that he had tissues to sell—as if the man couldn't see that—and then saying that the tissues were high quality, "soft and yet strong." He was probably smiling, which was the worst thing he could do.

Hadi, by then, was working his way up the outer lane. He was reaching lots of cars, not taking time to make an annoying sales pitch. But Hadi sold no chewing gum, and he got off the street as the cars started to move. When he and Malek met back at the corner, Malek was laughing. "I didn't sell anything. Did you?"

"No."

"Is it like that a lot?"

"Almost always."

"I'll figure it out. There must be a good way to do it. Why don't you say anything to the people?"

"It doesn't help. They either want what you sell or they don't."

"I can't believe that. There must be some good things to say."

This was going to be difficult. What Hadi missed already was time to sit on his stack of concrete blocks, time to let his mind go blank.

This was one of the busiest intersections in this part of the city, with businesses down the street to the west and more shops running off on a diagonal street to the north-west. Everything was congested west of this corner: too many cars, too many people walking in the traffic lanes because cars were parked on the sidewalks. That was why this corner was best.

When the cars stopped, the boys went back to their work. Hadi could still hear Malek begging the people, but his voice sounded happy, not miserable, even though he was now telling everyone that he had brothers and sisters who were hungry.

Hadi did manage to sell one package of gum. But when he turned to see how Malek was doing, he saw the boy step away from a car just as a scooter buzzed down the street between the lanes.

"Malek!" he shouted. "Watch out!"

Malek jumped back as the scooter shot by, missing him by only inches.

Hadi hurried to him. "I should have told you that," he said. "Never step out from the cars without looking. Scooters and motorcycles don't stay in lanes."

But Malek didn't seem fazed at all. "People in this country pay no attention to traffic laws, and the police don't seem to care," he said.

"There's a policeman on this corner sometimes—a man named Samir—and he blows his whistle and yells at people, but they pay no attention. He has no way to stop them and they know it."

Malek was laughing again. "Well, that was a close one," he said. "Thanks for looking out for me."

But Hadi didn't like that. He wasn't looking out for the boy. They weren't partners. They were just working on the same corner. And it was still Hadi's corner.

2

After a couple of hours, Hadi was beginning to think that Malek might not be a bad guy—except that he talked too much. The sound of his voice filled Hadi's brain. Hadi wanted time to himself after he approached a new round of drivers. He didn't like all the questions Malek kept asking.

As the afternoon dragged on, however, Hadi could tell that Malek was getting tired. He kept begging people to buy his tissues, but most of them ignored him. A few even yelled at him. Hadi remembered how all those insults had cut into him when he had first started. It had taken a long time to teach himself to shut all that out and just keep going until he found someone who would buy his gum. He knew he had changed over time. He didn't feel much anger—or happiness—but he got through his days, and he took a little money home every night.

But Malek was shocked by the rudeness he heard. "Some of the people call me names," he told Hadi.

"You can't listen to any of that," Hadi told him. "And don't say anything back to them. That only makes things worse."

Malek was nodding. "All right. Thanks. I'm glad you're here. I can learn a lot from you." Malek hesitated, seemed to think things over. "But some people aren't sure if they want to buy from me or not. I can see it when they look at me. I need to find the right thing to say to people like that."

Hadi shook his head. He wanted to tell Malek he didn't know what he was talking about. But maybe it was good for the kid to try something new. He would probably give up after a while and just do what Hadi did, but for now his days might turn out better than Hadi's.

Late in the afternoon, as the sun was sliding behind the buildings to the west, Malek finally said, "I haven't taken in enough money. I could be in trouble."

"What did that Kamal guy tell you?" Hadi asked. "How much money does he expect you to earn?"

"I'm not exactly sure."

But Hadi thought maybe Malek *was* sure. And from what Hadi had heard about these gang people, Kamal would take everything Malek earned today and leave him with nothing to take home. Hadi found himself feeling sorry for Malek, and he hadn't expected to feel anything like that.

For the first time all day Malek was quiet as he stood next to Hadi waiting for the cars to go by. "I thought I would sell more," he finally said.

"Kamal can't expect too much from you on your first day," Hadi told him. "You were only here half a day or so, and you can tell him you're trying to figure out what to say to people."

"You said it doesn't matter what I say."

"I know. But he doesn't know that."

"I guess that's right. So that's what I'll tell him. He'll understand that, don't you think?"

Hadi doubted that he would. But he said, "It's not your fault that you didn't earn more. You've worked hard."

Malek was nodding, probably rehearsing the words he would say to Kamal. "I've done my best," he muttered.

"That's right," Hadi told him.

But Hadi could only think that Malek knew nothing about the street, about people, especially nothing about men who sent kids to these corners and then took their money from them each night. The truth was, Hadi had hoped all day that Malek would fail, maybe even give up and get off his corner. But now he sensed how frightened Malek was. Hadi had never been forced to give his money to someone like Kamal, but he knew what it was like to go from car to car all day and end up with little to show for his work—knew how he felt when he saw in his mother's face that she was disappointed that she wouldn't have adequate food to pre-pare for her family.

Hadi took a big breath, tried not to feel too much. He couldn't help it if he hadn't had a great day either. He just hoped Baba, who sold items at another intersection, had done well, so their family could eat all right tonight. Lately, on these cold winter days, food had been sparse, and their apartment—their room—had been cold and miserable.

When the boys went back to the cars this time, Hadi didn't hear Malek say anything to the drivers. He moved quickly up the hill, keeping pace with Hadi. But neither boy sold anything, and when they returned to the corner, Malek said, "Why do people hate us so much, Hadi? When people look at me, even if they don't say anything, I can see that they hate me."

"They say there are too many Syrians in Lebanon, that we're ruining their country. My father says there really are too many of us. Like one or two million."

"But we lost our homes. We had to go somewhere."

"I know. But the people in Lebanon think we get all the help we need from the government—or from charities—and we don't need to bother them on the streets. That's not true. But they believe it."

"Why do they say we're dirty?"

"I don't know. Baba says it's easier to hate people if you think bad things about them."

Malek was shaking his head, looking confused.

"Malek, you've been in Lebanon awhile," Hadi told him. "Don't you know what people here think of us?"

"Sort of. But I didn't know that they were so angry. One man told me to move on or he would spit on me."

"I've heard that. I've heard everything."

Malek laughed. "At least he didn't do it. That's something to be thankful for."

Hadi turned and looked at Malek. He could hardly believe that the boy was still smiling.

Malek shrugged. "I always figure that things will get better after a while. They can't get any worse."

It had been a hard day for Malek. Hadi was impressed that he was still finding ways to keep his spirits up. "This is about the time I usually quit," he told Malek. "I meet my father before it's dark, and we ride home on a bus."

"I guess I'll quit too. I'll have to promise Kamal that I'll do better tomorrow."

"Where do you live?"

"It's called Bourj Hammoud. It's over that way." He pointed to the west.

"I know where it is. I walk through there to meet Baba."

So the two walked together. It was not what Hadi had thought would happen just a few hours earlier.

It was almost eight o'clock when Hadi and his father reached home. On the bus, Hadi told his father about Malek and about Kamal sending word that he should leave the corner. He tried not to sound too worried about it, but Baba told Hadi, "We might have to look for another place for you to work."

"I don't think we have to do that," Hadi told him. "We sort of worked things out so we can both stay."

"But be careful," Baba told him. "These street-gang bosses are dangerous people."

"Okay. I'll leave if I have to."

By the time Hadi and Baba got home, Hadi was very tired, but when they walked in, it was Mama who looked drained. "Where have you been?" she asked. "These children haven't eaten."

"The traffic was terrible," Baba told her. "I know we're late."

Hadi had stopped in Bourj Hammoud and bought some overripe fruit from his friend Garo, who operated a fruit and vegetable stand. He held up his net filled with apples and oranges, and his brothers and sisters ran to him. "An orange. I choose an orange," Khaled was yelling.

Hadi handed him one, but that set off a cry of protest. His three sisters were grabbing at the net, so he let them take it and tussle with one another over the other oranges and the apples. Little Aram, who was almost three, begged them for an apple, and Aliya gave him one that was half-rotten.

"Cut out the bad part," Hadi told his sisters. "It isn't right to give him that one. He doesn't understand which part he can eat."

They didn't listen, but Hadi knew how hungry they were, especially when they had waited until later than usual to eat. Aliya, who was seven, liked to boss her little sisters, but she was usually kind to Aram. After she took some bites of her apple, she found a knife in a drawer and cut his apple enough to salvage what she could. Aram didn't seem to care, as long as he had something. He was bundled up in a heavy coat—as everyone was. It was even colder than usual in the room. At least the charity organization in the neighborhood had made sure they all had heavy coats.

Rabia, who was six, and Samira, who was four, sat down together on the floor with blankets pulled around their legs and chomped on their apples. They also had an orange, which Aliya had told them to share. The floor was strewn with tangled blankets, but there was nothing else: no table like the one they had had in Syria long ago, no beds. It was just a room, mostly empty, with a little cookstove that ran on propane gas, which they bought in tanks. A blanket hung across the room dividing off a little section where Baba and Mama slept.

Hadi always forgot the smell of their apartment when he was out on the street all day, but it struck him when he came in at night. He didn't know exactly what it was: a hint of the toilets that were down the hall; probably mold from the incessant water leak that worked its way down one wall and spread onto the floor so everything felt damp all the time; and surely smells from little Jawdat, the baby. Mama washed his cloth diapers as best she could and reused them.

Mama was sitting quietly on the one chair in the room. Hadi picked up an apple that Aliya had left on the floor. He took it to a little counter by the sink, cut out the bad spots and sliced the apple into thin wedges, put them on a plate and carried them to his mother. He knew she couldn't bite into an apple. She had had a terrible toothache for more than a week now. Still, he thought she could eat the slices. She looked at him when he offered the plate, and he saw the appreciation in her eyes, but he also saw the pain. *"Chokran,"* she said, and she patted his hand. It was sometimes hard to see Mama behind her sadness, but he felt her affection in the little touch.

"Have you money to buy more food?" she asked.

"Yes. Some. I brought home—"

"We can't afford much," Baba said gently. "It's not been a good month for Hadi and me to make sales. We can buy a package or two of bread and some rice, but we have to keep out all we can for rent or on the first of the month we'll be out in the street."

Hadi watched his mother. She stared at her husband, didn't speak, and Hadi knew she was holding back what she was thinking. A few months back, she might have complained, but now she only looked beleaguered. What Hadi feared was that she was giving up.

Hadi wanted to tell his mother that all would be well, that she need not worry so much. He wanted to sound like Malek. But he couldn't get the words out. He watched her as she looked at Baba, her face strained with worry. She usually didn't wear her hijab over her head in the house, but she wore it now against the winter cold, and she wore her long black robe over heavy clothes. It made her look stout, but she wasn't. Her face was thin, all bones, her eyes hidden deep under her black eyebrows. Hadi remembered when people had told him how pretty his mother was, but they didn't say that now.

"Go, Hadi," Baba said. "Buy some food. Hurry." But he only gave Hadi eight thousand lira.

So Hadi headed for the door. He thought he could bargain for a little more than just the bread and rice, maybe some potatoes. "Come on, Khaled," he said. "Go with me."

So Khaled hurried to get his coat on. He always loved to go outside, or to do anything other than sit in the room. Hadi waited, and then, as they were walking down the dark flights of stairs, he said, "Khaled, I have something for you." He pulled the half sandwich from his jacket pocket. "It's cold now, but it will taste all right."

"A shawarma," Khaled said, as though Hadi had handed over a great treasure. And as soon as they were in the street, he bit into it and laughed at the same time.

"I know you don't get enough to eat," Hadi said. "Your little sisters can get by on what we give them, but you need more. You'll be starting to grow a lot before long."

"Thank you. Thank you." He was still chewing. When he swallowed, he said, "I am growing up. I want to go with you tomorrow—to your corner. I can earn some money and add it to what you and Baba take in. I want to do it."

Hadi had heard this all before. Khaled had begged over

and over to join Hadi and Baba in their work. Hadi understood how much Khaled hated being cooped up in the house with his sisters all day. But he also knew that Khaled wasn't ready for the streets. "You're too young."

"You were not much older than me when you started."

Hadi had no answer for that. He continued down the stairs and then stepped outside into the narrow street. Rain was falling again. He put his hood up. People were laughing nearby in a little stall where old men went to drink Turkish coffee and play cards. Another man across the street was closing up his electric supply shop, shutting bars over his door to lock out burglars. The smell was even worse out here, the stench of the sewer filling the air.

"This is not a good time to start," Hadi told Khaled. "There's a man who wants to take my corner away. He might beat up on me. I may have to run from him tomorrow and find another corner."

Khaled didn't seem to hear that. "It's terrible to stay home," he said. "The girls argue and Mama doesn't try to stop them. She wants me to watch Aram and Jawdat all the time, and I'm sick of doing that."

"Everything is very hard for Mama right now. Her tooth is hurting really bad."

"I know. Her face is swelling. But she's changed, Hadi. She used to play with us and think of things for us to do. Now she just sits, and sometimes she cries."

"She cries?"

"Yes. She doesn't want us to see, but we do."

Hadi felt a little sick. He had worried about his mother's toothache, but he hadn't known it was quite so bad. Sometimes the pain and the mounting problems for his family seemed more than he could bear to think about.

"That's why I want to work," Khaled said. "If I earn even a little, we can save it up, and Baba can take her to a dentist."

Hadi had thought the same thing. He and Baba had even talked about it. They understood that Khaled wanted to be a man, but they also knew that he wasn't ready to face people in cars cursing him and telling him he was filthy.

"No, Khaled. Not yet. But it's good you want to help."

"Baba said we'll be kicked out of our house next month."

"No. He said we could be. But we eat something every day. And we always manage to pay the rent. It's all we can do for now. But don't worry. We'll be all right."

"What if you lose your corner?"

Yes. That was the problem. Hadi doubted he could earn as much money if he moved to another intersection—one that no one else wanted. He felt fear pressing on his chest, had felt it almost constantly lately. But today, since Malek had arrived and told Hadi that a man named Kamal wanted to take his corner away, he had felt as though he couldn't get enough breath into his lungs.

3

On the following morning, Hadi hoped that Malek wouldn't come and he could have his corner to himself again. But Malek did show up, and not just the next morning, but each day after that. Hadi didn't know whether Kamal knew that he and Malek were working on the same corner. What he feared was that Kamal would spot him still there, or maybe send someone to spy on them. Hadi looked around at times, trying to spot someone watching them. If that happened, he worried what Kamal would do to him.

But a week passed and nothing changed. By then Hadi had begun to like having Malek around. He sometimes missed having time to sit on his concrete blocks to let his mind drift away from the tediousness of his day, but he was finding it was actually better to talk with Malek, laugh with him, and not be alone. The two kept learning more about each other, and Hadi was finding out that some things about their lives had been much the same.

One afternoon, with a drizzle of rain falling, they stood in their usual spot and waited for the cars to stop. Malek asked Hadi, "How many years were you in school before you came to Lebanon?"

The subject had come up before, but Hadi had avoided a clear answer. He decided now that he might as well admit the truth. "Our school got hit by a bomb when I was in second grade. So that was the last year for me. By then the city was all blown apart. In our part of the city, no schools were open."

"But I guess you at least learned to read."

"Yes. Some," Hadi said, "but I haven't had much chance to practice since then." He knew he hadn't learned much at all. Before the schools closed, the siege had begun and all supplies from outside the city had been cut off. Aleppo had been under almost constant attack with barrel bombs and cluster bombs falling. The continuous distress had only been broken by periods of terrible panic. Hadi remembered the thunder of bombs and the flash of the explosions that, even when fairly distant, made concentration almost impossible. Eventually, most of the buildings on his street had looked like skeletons, partly blown away but still standing. He had never stopped worrying that the next bomb would hit his building. Maybe Malek understood what that was like; maybe he didn't.

"Next year I'm going to school," Hadi told Malek. "My father promised me." And it was true about the promise. But Baba had made the same promise the year before. Once, the foreign couple had parked their car and walked to his corner. They had asked him whether he attended a school. Hadi had told them that he didn't, and as best he could understand, they had said they could get him into a school. He had wanted to take them up on their offer, but he couldn't. He didn't think they had fully understood what he tried to explain. But without the money he earned each day, his family wouldn't be able to eat.

"I'm a good reader," Malek said. "And I'm even better in mathematics. I got high grades in every subject. I did very well in English, too, and I learned some French. My teachers always told me how smart I was."

Hadi had gotten used to Malek bragging this way, but he'd realized there was something sad about it—as though Malek clung fast to the idea that his life would get better at some point. He kept saying that someday he would be an engineer like his father. Hadi didn't think Malek could ever do that, but he sort of liked hearing him talk about it. It was nice to imagine that better times might be ahead for both of them.

"So, why do you want to be an engineer?" Hadi asked.

"My father always talks about it. He says an engineer thinks up ideas, draws them on paper, and then those ideas turn into real things—buildings or cars, or anything. Everything you see, someone had to picture it in his mind first."

"I guess that's right," Hadi said. He even liked the idea. But he was almost certain that it was useless to hope for such possibilities. Maybe Hadi and Malek could get jobs someday—some sort of work the Lebanese didn't want to do—but how were they supposed to attend a university? And who would hire them if they did?

"I'm going to do it, Hadi. I'm not going to give up, no matter what."

"Maybe things will change," Hadi said, and that seemed the best he could offer.

"Sure. Things will probably change before too much longer. The war might end, for one thing. That would help."

Baba had told Hadi that the war in Syria was nowhere close to ending. But Hadi decided not to say that.

"So, Hadi, what kind of work do you want to do?" Malek asked.

Hadi glanced up the street. Instead of answering, he said, "The cars are stopping."

So the boys worked the cars again. Malek hadn't quite given up entirely on trying to make a sales pitch for his tissues. When windows were open, he would still try to smile and say something to the drivers. Hadi heard him say, "I want to go to a university when I'm older. You can help me save for that."

Hadi looked over to see one of the drivers, a young, rather shabby-looking man, laugh at Malek. He said something Hadi couldn't hear, but Malek told the man, "I'll still do it. My mind's made up."

The man kept laughing, and he didn't buy any tissues, but Hadi found himself admiring Malek for admitting to his hope. Maybe it was good to tell these people that they weren't just stupid street kids, even if it didn't help to sell tissues.

Hadi made a few more sales that afternoon—and accepted money from two people who didn't take the gum. He had taken in 9,500 pounds with a couple of hours still to go. If he could pick up a few thousand more, he'd please his father at the end of the day.

Malek, though, was still not doing as well. He didn't tell Hadi how much he had earned, but Hadi hadn't seen him sell much of anything.

When the boys were back on their corner later in the day, Malek said, "You never answered me. What kind of work do you want to do when you grow up?"

"I don't know."

"There must be something you've thought of—something you've seen people do. What kind of work did your father do in Syria?"

"He was a truck driver."

"Truck drivers do quite well, I think. Maybe you could do that."

"Maybe. I guess that would be all right."

"You don't sound excited about it. What would you do if you could get any job you've ever heard about?"

Hadi was embarrassed to answer, but he said, "When I was little—back in Syria—I saw this TV show one time. It told all about astronauts—how they flew to the moon and all those things. I told Baba that's what I wanted to do.

I wanted to fly to the moon or maybe to another planet, like Mars." He laughed at himself. He knew the idea was silly. "Baba told me, if that's what you want to do, you should try. Maybe it could happen."

"That's right. Your father gave you good advice. If you keep trying, you may not become an astronaut, but you might be a scientist of some kind. You could study the stars and everything."

"It's called an 'astronomer.' I remember that. I had a book that my father read to me. It was about traveling into space. My baba brought it home to me after I told him about the show I'd seen on TV. The book had that word in it—astronomer."

Hadi ached at the memory. It brought back thoughts of his nice apartment before the bombing had become so bad: his living room, Baba sitting next to him on the couch. Good things—a good future—had seemed possible then. Baba was not the same man anymore. He still tried to be kind, but he no longer spoke of days ahead, better or not; everything was about food for the day, rent for the month. He never stopped worrying that the family would end up out on the street or forced to live in tin and cardboard shacks the way many refugees did. Hadi also knew how much it pained Baba that he still hadn't taken Mama to a dentist.

"You remembered the word 'astronomer' after all these years?" Malek asked.

"Yes." Hadi had been little then. He tried to think how

he had felt about everything. It had been like choosing a future that would magically happen. He had looked at that book about stars, and he had put the stars in his head, and for a long time they had stayed. But the bombs had exploded them, and the days on the street had blacked them out.

"I think you're smart, Hadi. I think we both are. And I think we'll both be successful."

Hadi had sat for so many months on those concrete blocks, just trying not to feel anything. It was good to think that something better might come. Malek didn't understand much about working on the street, about the Lebanese, about things that were simply impossible, but he brought back something to Hadi: that way of thinking that Baba had offered him early in his life. Hadi knew he wasn't a child, that he had been forced to grow up, but he longed for that time when happiness has seemed the normal way of things.

Clouds had been drifting in, turning dark. Hadi knew there would be rain before the day ended and, most likely, continuing into the morning. Malek had noticed the clouds too, and he had begun to glance at the sky nervously. "The rainy days stop in a month or two," Hadi told him. "And the weather is nice for a while. People always buy more on nice days."

Since starting to share the corner with Hadi, Malek had seen mostly rainy, cold days, and Hadi knew that in spite of Malek's optimism about the distant future, he was actually worried every day about his failure to earn more money. He had had a few good days—maybe one or two—when he had taken in a decent amount of money, but most of his days had been disappointing.

Malek glanced toward Hadi and nodded. He seemed to appreciate the scrap of encouragement. "What about summer?"

"Hot," Hadi said. "But not hot like Syria. It was much hotter for you in Damascus, I think. Here, it's not so bad."

"That's good." They nodded again, and then they went back to the cars. Hadi had not wanted to be partners with Malek, but it felt a little that way now. He kept telling himself that he didn't want any of Malek's hope. It only led to disappointment. But since Malek had shown up, Hadi really did feel more alive. It was a strange partnership the two were forming, but Hadi felt himself giving in to it.

Another week went by and Hadi felt encouraged. He and Malek were getting along fine, and Hadi didn't think he had lost many of his sales by sharing his corner. But one Monday morning in the middle of February, Malek seemed troubled. He wouldn't look at Hadi, and even though the day was warm and clear, he kept his hood up, tied tight around his chin. "Aren't you getting hot?" Hadi asked him. Hadi had already taken his jacket off.

Malek took a long look at Hadi, then untied his hood and pushed it back. Hadi saw a deep scratch across Malek's cheek and a cut on his ear. "What happened?" Hadi asked.

"I need to start bringing home more money," Malek said. "Kamal came over on Sunday afternoon, and he started telling my father that I wasn't working hard enough. He got really mad at me. He swung at me with the back of his hand. His wristwatch caught the side of my head."

"Who? Kamal?"

Malek hesitated, but then he nodded.

"Doesn't he know you've been out here trying all day, every day?"

Malek drew in some air and looked at the ground. "I found out that Kamal has an assistant—a guy who walks around to watch all the kids who sell for him. On Saturday that guy told Kamal that sometimes you and I stand here and talk after the cars have stopped."

"We don't do that!"

"I remember once when we did. We still got out there, but not as fast as we could have."

"So what's he saying you have to do?"

"He says you have to leave so that I have the corner to myself. If you don't, he said to warn you that he'll come after you. He was really angry. I think he means it."

Hadi stared at Malek. He was trying to decide whether he had any options.

"But I don't know," Malek said. "If I have a few good days, maybe he'll forget all about it."

"There are always good days and bad days, Malek. That doesn't have anything to do with me."

"I know. And you've taught me some things I needed to know. I tried to tell him that, but he wouldn't listen."

But Hadi needed his corner.

"I was thinking," Malek said, "maybe you could cross the street and work over there by the cabstand. You could take the traffic going north, and I would stay here, where cars go west. I don't know what he can say about that. It's not the same corner."

"I'm not leaving, Malek. I told you that the first day you came here. I need to be where people know me. And I don't want to put up with those cabbies over there."

"But if I cross the street, he won't accept that."

There were no good choices. Hadi felt his chest tighten, his fear come back. For a couple of weeks he had been breathing a little better. "Let's just see what happens. If you have any really bad days, I could lend you some money and you could pay me back when you have a better day than I do. We could even things out that way."

Now it was Malek who was staring at Hadi. "You would do that?"

Hadi was surprised at himself that he had made such an offer, but he didn't dare cross the street. If his income dropped drastically over there, he would be worse off than if he lent some money to Malek from time to time.

"That really might help," Malek said. "But I can't believe you would—"

"Okay then, that's what we'll do."

"But there has to be something I could do for you."

"No, you don't have to do that. It's just—"

"I could help you improve your reading. If you could bring something with you—a book or a magazine—I could help you with the words you don't know. I could teach you a few words every day and you'll start improving really fast."

"All right," Hadi said. "We can try it. But we can't stand here looking at a book very long—or we'll be in trouble again."

"I know. But we could do a new word every now and then, just while we're standing here at the corner."

The two boys looked at each other for just a moment, and then they both nodded. They had a deal.

What occurred to Hadi was that he finally had a friend in Lebanon. In Syria, after his school had been demolished, he had felt cut off from his friends. There was a day, now and then, when no bombing raids had come, and he had faced dreary times with nothing to do. He and some other boys had found an open space in their neighborhood where grass was still growing. They had cleared away rubble and had played soccer, sometimes all day long. One boy had a ball, but it wouldn't hold air very long, so they had used an old bicycle pump to keep it inflated as best they could, and soccer had been the right thing in Hadi's life at the time. He wasn't very good at the game, couldn't run as fast, couldn't control the ball as well as some of the boys, but no one cared. No one even kept score. They ran hard, used up their energy,

DEAN HUGHES

and they laughed all they could. Every boy seemed Hadi's best friend.

But Hadi couldn't fight back another image he tried never to think about. A little girl named Marwa, only five or so, had come to the soccer games with her brother Mohammad. He told her to watch the boys play, but little Marwa wanted to play too. The older boys had let her play. They had laughed at her efforts, but they liked her happiness. After that, she came whenever the boys played, and everyone liked her. Then one day, after a raid on their neighborhood, Hadi had seen Mohammad sitting in the street with his mother. She was holding a little body, all covered in dust and dirt. The body was twisted, the legs bent wrong. Mohammad was sobbing, holding a little hand and saying, "I love you, Marwa. I love you." But Hadi could see that Marwa was dead. He turned and ran, hid away in his bedroom so no one would see, and he cried and cried, couldn't stop. He tried now never to think of that day, but it was always with him.

Hadi pushed the thought aside, and the boys kept working. He was pleased that the better weather seemed to improve the mood of the drivers. By midafternoon Malek said he had taken in more than he ever had in one day, and he made a few more sales after that. Hadi could only think that Kamal would now ease off on his warnings. His breath came a little easier.

4

The daylight was lasting a little longer now, but as the sun was getting low in the sky, Hadi and Malek walked into Bourj Hammoud toward the Dora intersection, where Baba sold his items each day. It was the part of town where Malek lived, a section where only Armenians had lived at one time but was now more mixed.

As they walked together, Malek asked, "How can you and your father afford to take a bus to go home?"

"It costs us each a thousand lira, each way, but there's no place to sell anything in our neighborhood and it's too far to walk all the way over here."

"Where is your neighborhood exactly?"

"It's called Cola. It's on the east side of the city." Hadi didn't want to admit what a stinking place it was, with crumbling concrete buildings, worn and faded canvas sunshades, and narrow alleys strung with huge bunches of electrical wires that drooped and twisted in all directions.

　　　　　　　　　　　　　　　　　　　　　　　DEAN HUGHES

The alleys were thick with people, scooters, and delivery trucks. Garbage was everywhere, the smell of it always in the air. Old men were usually playing cards in front of little cafés—drinking, and sometimes shouting at one another. And children played in the middle of all this, pretending they were soldiers with sticks for guns.

"Do you have a nice place to live?" Malek asked.

"No. It's just one room," Hadi said, but he didn't want to describe his empty, smelly apartment. He was sure that Malek's family didn't live in quite such degrading conditions.

"That's what we have too," Malek said. "Just one room."

"For how many?"

Malek thought for a few seconds, as though he needed to count, and then he said, "Eight. The building isn't too bad, really, but we're very crowded."

Hadi hadn't expected that answer. Maybe things weren't any better for Malek's family than they were for Hadi's. "How did you and your brothers get started with Kamal?" Hadi asked. Malek had told him before that he had two older brothers, and they were all doing the same work.

"Kamal lives in our neighborhood. He talked to my father one day and told him he would supply tissues for us to sell and give us good corners. He promised he would look out for us, make sure no one beat up on us or anything like that."

"My father and I chose our own corners," Hadi said. "It costs us four thousand a day to come over here, but we don't have to pay anyone at the end of the day. And no one's ever tried to take our places away . . . until now."

"Kamal told us he's taking control of all the intersections around here. He said that no one would dare go against him from now on."

When they came to the corner where Malek and Hadi separated each day, Hadi asked, "Do you have rats in your building, or leaking water, and things like that?"

"No. It's not like that. But Baba is worried. He says that if we don't bring home more money, we'll have to look for something cheaper."

"If he finds a job, can't you—"

"He won't find a job, Hadi. It's just what he always says. I don't think he even tries anymore. He's not *really* an engineer. Not exactly. He worked *for* an engineer in Syria, and he did the things engineers do. But he didn't go to college. And even if he had, no one would hire him here in Lebanon. He had a job when we first came here—a labor job—but he had an accident and he can't do that kind of work anymore."

The boys were standing in the half-light, cars buzzing past them, a draft of cold air whisking over them. The weather was taking another turn. Malek pulled his hood over his head, and then Hadi did too.

"When we got here last year, my father looked for engineering jobs and a man told him that he didn't need engineers, but he would hire him to lay concrete blocks on a big building project. He did that for a few months and I was able to go to school. But then a worker dropped a block on my father's hand and broke some of the bones. His hand is still bad, and no one will hire him to lay blocks now. The man he worked for just said, 'I need men with two hands. I can't keep a man on the job who can't do the work.'"

Hadi had heard stories like that before. There was no protection for people who worked for cash. And they couldn't afford to get good medical care.

"My father's frustrated, and he takes it out on my brothers and me," Hadi said. "He's angry every day no matter how much we bring home. He listens to Kamal, who tells him that we aren't working hard enough. Especially me. My father curses me. Tells me I'm worthless." Malek looked down at the sidewalk, and Hadi knew he was trying to get control of his emotions. "I wasn't going to tell you any of this stuff, but . . . I guess things are pretty bad for you, too."

Hadi also looked down. He noticed a twisted break in the sidewalk, the crack filled with dirt and cigarette butts. He wondered why everything had to be so dirty, so broken apart. "My mother has a toothache," he said. "Baba can't afford to take her to a dentist. He asks my mother every day if she can wait a little longer, and she always says she can. But she's in pain all the time. She doesn't complain, but she's turned silent, like she's not even with us anymore."

"Does she take care of your little brothers and sisters?"

"Yes. But my sisters make her crazy with all their noise. Mama doesn't even try to stop them anymore. One of my sisters—Aliya—causes trouble on purpose. She gets louder when Mama asks her to be quiet. And she gets my other sisters in trouble."

"Doesn't Aliya understand about your mother's toothache?"

"I guess she does. But my sisters and my little brothers are in that room all day every day. There's no place to play outside, and the neighborhood is dangerous. Our electricity goes off a lot, so everyone's in the dark about half the time."

"It's kind of the same for my little brothers and sisters. They have nowhere to go, nothing to do. They end up fighting with each other."

Hadi looked up from the sidewalk into Malek's eyes. "So anyway, things are kind of the same for both of us."

"Yes." Malek was nodding, but he was quick to add, "Hadi, my father was a different man back in Syria. He was happy, not angry."

"And in Syria, Mama was fun. She was brave, even during bombing raids. We would go to the basement and she would get us all to sing old Syrian songs. And before the siege, we used to go to her village and see my grandparents and all my uncles and aunts and cousins. Everyone would laugh together—and eat and eat and eat. All that's gone now. She has nothing to hope for."

"It's my father who has changed the most," Malek said. "He brought money with him from Syria, and he built up savings when he was working here. But now he's lost his strong hands. He's scared as he watches our money get used up."

Hadi couldn't think of anything to say.

"It wasn't Kamal who hit me," Malek said.

"Pardon me?"

"It was my father. Kamal said I wasn't working hard. But he wasn't the one who hit me. After Kamal left, my father meant to slap me with the back of his hand, but his wristwatch dug into my ear. He was sorry, afterward."

Hadi understood. The two stood a little longer, even though the rain was falling harder now.

"We can't give up," Malek said. "We have to do what we can, keep trying, and somehow things will get better."

Hadi didn't really believe that things would get better. But he didn't say that.

"Hadi, you still might have to work on the other side of the street. I made good money today, but it feels like the rain is coming back. I might do worse tomorrow. Kamal might get really angry if he finds out you're still working on the corner with me."

Hadi knew he couldn't put Malek in danger. He took a breath and then said, "All right. I'll cross the street tomorrow."

"But if you leave the corner, don't leave the intersection, and bring a book if you can. Or something else you can learn some words from."

"All right." But Hadi felt sick. He didn't think he could

do well on the other side of the street and he hated to think that Kamal had won.

"I'll see you in the morning," Malek said.

It was what he had said each night as the two had parted ways, but it felt different this time. The boys seemed to have a new understanding of each other. Hadi gave Malek a pat on the back, and then he watched as Malek crossed the street and headed down the narrow side street that was crowded with parked cars on the sidewalks.

Hadi continued his long walk toward the Dora intersection. Light rain had begun to fall and the air felt colder, but Hadi liked the busyness of Bourj Hammoud, with all its stores along the streets. There were shops selling jewelry, clothing, hardware—everything—and street vendors selling pastries, ice cream, falafel sandwiches. And, of course, there was Garo's fruit and vegetable stand, where Hadi stopped every night. He was always glad to see the old man, and Garo seemed to like seeing him. "How are you today, Garo?" Hadi asked when he reached the stand.

Garo smiled, his big white mustache arching upward over brown teeth. "I'm cold," he said. "Too cold. I was never cold when I was young like you. Now I'm always cold—even in summer." He nodded, laughed, pulled an old gray baseball cap down a little tighter on his head. He was under a canvas cover, where the rain didn't hit him. He was a hefty, round man who stayed in his seat most of the time and usually told customers to gather up what they wanted and bring everything to him. Hadi was sure that Garo didn't like to pull himself out of the chair any more often than he had to. "Step in, Hadi," he said. "Don't stand there and get wet."

Hadi did step closer. "Do you have anything I can buy from you today?"

"Yes, of course."

Garo had some apples ready again today, bagged up, and he told Hadi, "I have some bananas that are a little too ripe, a nice big cabbage you could strip the outer leaves from, or lots of potatoes that are getting too old to sell."

"I'll take the apples and the potatoes," Hadi said. He knew that potatoes filled up stomachs about as well as anything.

Hadi tried to give Garo two five-hundred-pound coins, but Garo took only one. And he said, "I'm putting three pomegranates in your net. I think your brothers and sisters will like that."

"Oh no, Garo, you can't—"

"Don't tell me what I can do and can't do. They're a gift. Enjoy them."

Hadi was actually thrilled. That meant Hadi had lots of food to take home and he still had 14,500 pounds for his day. That was good, even though he had had a few better days lately.

"Thank you," Hadi said. *"Allah yehmik."*

"Yes, thank you, my friend. I'll take my blessings where I can get them. I don't suppose Allah minds blessing a Christian now and then."

Hadi laughed. Sometimes he wondered about God. He knew there were lots of Christians in this part of the city, and some of his friends in Syria had also been Christians, but he didn't understand exactly what the difference was between them and Muslims, or why some people in one religion hated those in another. But Garo wasn't like that. What Hadi knew was that Garo liked him. And he liked Garo.

Hadi shook hands with Garo, thanked him again, and he felt happy as he walked away.

By the time Hadi reached his father, the rain was falling harder and the streets were gleaming with the reflecting lights from the cars' headlights. He found his father under an awning. "You're late, Hadi," Baba said. "I was worried about you."

"I talked to Malek after work for a few minutes, and I stopped to buy some things from Garo."

"That's good. How much money do you have for us today?"

"Fourteen thousand, five hundred. But also apples, potatoes, and three pomegranates."

"That's good. The children will like that." Hadi liked seeing the satisfaction in his father's face. "I took in a little more than you, but not as much profit. People take one look at these umbrellas and know they aren't worth much. They all want to bargain with me."

Baba sold lots of different things. He went to the back room of a shop each morning and bought items he thought people might want. In summer it was sunglasses or covers for steering wheels. Now, in winter, he sold umbrellas or rain hats, or sometimes gloves. He often ended up with little to show for his day's work. But people wouldn't buy gum from a grown man. He had to offer something that people actually wanted to have. Besides, Hadi knew that Baba couldn't stay home and send him out on the streets. He was always hoping for a real job, but he had to do whatever he could.

"Are things still all right on your corner?" Baba asked. "You've heard nothing from the street gang?"

"Nothing so far. I think Kamal gets angry sometimes, and then he forgets about me again. I told Malek I would cross the street tomorrow and work by the cabstand."

Hadi saw the concern in his father's face. But Baba only said, "I hope that's good enough for Kamal. If he threatens you again, you'll have to leave." He considered for a moment and then added, "Let's cross over to our bus stop. We need to get home. We'll talk on the bus."

So they walked together. Hadi didn't like hearing his father sound so fearful. Baba was not old, not like Garo, but it bothered Hadi that he seemed to be aging, especially this winter. The cold outside—and the cold in their apartment— seemed to be taking something out of him. Or maybe it was the worry about paying the rent. Baba was not a big man, but he had always seemed strong to Hadi. He had muscular arms and hands, could always lift almost anything, but some of the firmness, the confidence had gone out of his eyes, and he had stopped shaving. His beard grew in weak clumps, and gray was filling up his hair. Lines were forming around his eyes. The worst part was, his face always seemed serious, even somber, now. Hadi remembered when he had liked to joke with Hadi and his siblings, but now he rarely smiled.

They waited on a corner of the big roundabout intersection while rain beat down on them and they turned their backs to the wind. A bus—one with a deep, rusty scratch down the side—finally stopped, and Hadi and Baba got on. They each paid 1,000 pounds, and now Hadi had only 13,500 for his day. It was the same every day, but this was the cheapest kind of bus, and it took a long way around to get to their part of town.

They sat next to each other, toward the front, on plastic seats that were worn and cracked. The bus rattled and swayed, and the noise of the engine was like a pump that hadn't been greased, squealing and surging.

"Hadi," Baba said, keeping his voice low, "Kamal's gang is taking this side of Beirut. Everyone's talking about it, and now I see it for sure. These people are not afraid to kill. And the police do nothing about it. I think it's time for you to find a corner that the gang doesn't want."

Hadi was sitting by the window. He looked out to the busy street, the mass of cars, none of them staying in lanes. The drivers were all pressing in on one another, edging left or right, trying to force their way ahead any way they could.

And everyone was honking. It was the same every night at this time, but it was always worse when it rained. The whole mess out there made Hadi tired. It would be late before they got home.

"If I work on the other side of the street, maybe everything will be okay."

"Maybe it's not worth it, Hadi. Maybe we should look for another corner for you tomorrow—one closer to me."

But Hadi didn't want to do that. "I'll go back in the morning and I'll work on the other side of the street. A lot of the same people come by over there—just at different times of the day."

"All right. But if this Kamal guy comes around, you'll have to clear out. Don't talk back to him."

"Okay." But Hadi told himself he wasn't going to leave unless he had no other choice. He didn't say it to Baba, but Hadi wanted to talk to Malek as often as he could. He thought maybe he could cross the street a time or two each day, at least long enough to learn a few new words.

The bus gradually worked its way through the worst of the traffic and crawled toward the southwest side of Beirut. Hadi could see the downtown area, the last of the sun making silhouettes of the tall buildings. He could see lights in many of the windows and knew that people must still be there, up on those high floors. Baba had told him that some of the buildings were apartment houses and some were hotels. But others were office buildings, where people had good jobs. It was never entirely clear to him what people in offices did all day, but he knew to get jobs like that, people had to be good readers. Hadi wasn't sure that Malek was right, that the two of them could do all the things they imagined themselves doing, but for now he felt sure the one thing he could do was improve his reading. And if he left the intersection in Bauchrieh and couldn't spend any time with Malek, he didn't know how he could manage it.

As the bus passed by businesses, he tried to read the signs. When he saw what kind of store it was and then looked at the Arabic letters, he usually realized what the word must be. But many of the signs were in English, and some probably in French, and he didn't know those letters. That was something else he would have to learn.

It was late again when Baba and Hadi reached home. When they walked in, all the children jumped up. At least Hadi had apples again, and that was something they could eat immediately. It was the potatoes that would have to fill them, but it was the apples they loved. He held back the pomegranates for the moment, knowing how happy they would make everyone.

5

That night Hadi and his family ate the same as usual: potatoes and bread. But the pomegranates had been a great surprise. The girls loved pulling the fruit apart and savoring
the sour, sweet seeds one at a time. Mama liked the taste
of them too; she even smiled at Hadi as she thanked him.

Mama had fed the family better in Syria. Hadi remembered tabbouleh, kibbeh, fattoush, falafel, and above all,
the creamy, rich hummus and baba ghanoush they had
eaten with their bread. He remembered roasted meat,
especially lamb, but his brothers and sisters had no rec-
ollection of such food. They had been too young—or not
yet born.

Hadi knew that it hurt his mother not to have good food
to prepare. She tried to make the best of things by adding
a few spices to bland foods, but all this winter, with Baba
and Hadi's income more limited, she had stopped asking
for cumin or za'atar. Or maybe she had realized that no

one noticed what she did with the food. They were all too hungry to care.

Baba had also given up on some of the things he had done in Syria. He didn't pray very often, rarely went to the mosque, usually worked on Friday. He still fasted during Ramadan, but that had become his usual way anyway, to eat only two meals a day, one early, one late. He still spoke of God, still told Mama and the children that things would get better, "*inshallah*," but Hadi heard a difference in his voice. It was harder and harder to trust in God when everything kept getting worse, not better.

By the time dinner was over, the electricity had gone off. In the dark, the children quarreled about the scattered blankets. "That's *my* blanket," Aliya kept saying. "Give it to me."

But Rabia wouldn't listen. "Find another one," she shouted.

Hadi hated to hear such ugliness between his sisters. When his siblings had been babies, he had loved holding them and then playing with them as they began to recognize him. He had cared for the older ones each time new babies had been born, and he had been especially close to his three cute little dark-eyed sisters. But that was all before he had gone to the streets with Baba. It pained him now to watch Aliya become so unkind, so belligerent, and to watch the other girls fight back against her bossiness. And poor Aram was so little that he knew nothing but this room, this darkness, this gloom.

The girls quieted after a time, even hugged together for warmth, their angry fight forgotten. Hadi rolled up in a corner with just one blanket, his feet cold. But he fell asleep quickly.

Early in the morning he was aware that he had awakened many times, each time trying to wrap his blanket tighter around him. All the same, he longed to stay in his corner all day. He pulled the blanket closer and slept a little more.

But then, only a few minutes later, Baba was there, shaking his shoulder even though there was not yet any light coming in from outside. "I'm sorry," he said, "but we have to get up and get ready." Hadi struggled to his feet. He walked down the hallway to the smelly toilet, and then he came back and ate some rice they had saved from the night before. He tried to leave most of it for the little ones. He would get by. Maybe the foreigners would bring him a shawarma sandwich again.

Hadi and his father rode the bus silently that morning. It bounced and rattled, and Hadi let himself sway from side to side as he tried to sleep. When he and his father got off at the Dora intersection, Baba said, "Hadi, don't take any chances today. If Malek thinks you have to leave, just do it."

"But we need to earn all we can. Mama needs—"

"I know. I have to find a way to get some help for her." He put his hand on Hadi's shoulder and waited until Hadi looked up at him. "But I have to think of you, too. You're young, son, and I'm asking too much of you as it is. You can't sacrifice yourself. Promise me you'll leave if you see any sign of danger."

"All right. I promise."

They were standing on a corner, the cars locked in a struggle to get through the big roundabout, many of the drivers honking, shouting, with pedestrians cutting through the mash of traffic and scooters winding their way between the cars. It was the usual thing and yet more bothersome this morning. Hadi didn't really feel awake yet, but he had taken a last look at Mama as he had left—and at Khaled. They had both seemed lost. Hopeless.

Hadi didn't want to spend the day looking for a new corner. He would not only lose a day's earnings; he would end up someplace where he would surely bring in less money. He also wanted to be with Malek. So he tried to think of some other answer. "Maybe Khaled should come with us now," Hadi told his father in spite of what he had told his brother. "He could help us a little."

"Not until you know what's going to happen. When Khaled starts, I want him to start with you, but we can't add another boy to your intersection with this Kamal already trying to push you away."

Hadi nodded. He knew that was true.

"It's not raining," Baba said. "Maybe we'll do better." And then he added, as always, *"Inshallah."*

Hadi wished Allah's blessing for prosperity on his father,

and then he walked through Bourj Hammoud. When he reached Garo's stand, the old man was setting up for the day. "Can I help you with those boxes?" Hadi asked him.

Garo set down a box of avocados, then turned to look at Hadi. He smiled. "Good morning, Hadi," he said. "Thank you, but . . ." He stopped, glanced toward the back of his stand. "Actually, you could help me with those melons back there. The box is a little big for me."

"Sure I will," Hadi said, and he was thrilled to do something for Garo. He had offered many times, but Garo had always said he could manage by himself. So Hadi lifted one end of the box, Garo the other, and they carried it to a table at the front of the stand.

"Thanks so much, my friend," Garo said. "You're a strong boy. You made the lift easy for me."

"Any time you need help, just tell me."

Garo patted Hadi gently on the shoulder. "I will, Hadi. I will. But I can do the rest. You go on to your place now. And have a good day."

Hadi smiled at him. "You too," he said.

"*Inshallah*," Garo said, and they both laughed.

Hadi felt more awake after that, and he walked a little faster the rest of the way. The rain had stopped, but the traffic, the noise, the people on the streets—it was all the same. So he worked his way through the traffic on the way to his corner, and he told himself that Kamal seemed to be all talk, that he wouldn't bother to chase Hadi off the corner. What he was remembering was that he had promised to bring something that he and Malek could read, so he watched along the way for a newspaper that someone might have tossed aside.

Not far from his intersection in Bauchrieh was a store that sold paper and pens and other such things, and it also sold books. He hadn't managed to find a newspaper, but when he passed the bookstore, he wondered what books cost. He stopped just to look in the window, and when he did, a book cover caught his eye. On it was a picture of an astronaut, dressed in a space suit, standing on the surface of the moon, just as Hadi had once imagined himself doing. He tried to read the title. He recognized "first" and "moon," but he couldn't decipher the other words. He thought maybe he could save a coin or two each day, and after a time buy the book. But he put the thought aside instantly. Right now all his money had to go to getting help for Mama.

As he was still standing at the window, two boys came out of the store. They were about his age, or maybe a little older. They were Lebanese, he thought, probably on their way to school, and maybe they had stopped to buy a notebook or a pencil. "Can you tell me something?" he asked one of the boys. He was embarrassed to ask them, but he really wanted to know.

The boy was short and soft, with fat cheeks. He had been laughing about something, but now he looked surprised. "Excuse me?" he said.

"Could you tell me what the words say on that book?"

Both boys laughed. "Don't you know?"

Hadi took a breath. "No." He looked past the boy.

"Can't you read?"

Hadi should have known they would make fun of him. He turned to walk away.

"It says 'American Astronauts: First Landing on the Moon.'"

Hadi looked back, nodded. "Thank you," he said.

"You must be a Syrian."

Hadi wasn't going to have this conversation. But he didn't want to be shamed. On impulse, he said, "I think I'll buy that book," and he reversed himself and stepped to the door.

The Lebanese boys laughed harder, and Hadi knew it had been a stupid thing to say. He hadn't avoided any shame; they knew he couldn't read. Still, he walked in, and inside the little shop, he found the shelves where the books were displayed. He looked for more copies of the book about the men who had landed on the moon, but he couldn't see any. He knew that a woman was behind a glass counter, off to his right, and he felt it would look strange merely to turn around and walk back out, so he pulled a book from the shelf, looked at the cover, and then began to turn some of the pages. The book had no picture on the front, and he couldn't find many words he knew. But he wasn't concentrating; he was mostly worried about the woman, who was watching him intently.

He kept turning the pages, and he acted as though he were stopping here and there to read a passage. He was ready to put the book back and make his way out of the store when the woman said, "Don't try to slip that book inside your jacket."

Hadi was taken by surprise. He had glanced at the woman when he had walked in, and she looked rather nice. She was an older woman, older than his mother, with gray hair and with round eyeglasses. He hadn't expected her to sound so stern. "Excuse me?" he asked.

"I know you can't read that book. What you can do is steal it and then try to sell it. It's happened in here before."

Hadi couldn't think what to say.

"You're a street boy. I've seen you on the corner begging people to give you money."

Hadi thought of saying that he didn't beg; he *sold* chewing gum. But it was probably all the same to her. He wasn't going to talk to her. He turned and slid the book back onto the shelf, exactly in the spot where he had found it.

"You Syrian children will steal anything. The government gives you food and clothes. You have more than the Lebanese children. But you aren't satisfied. You have to grab for more."

Hadi finally looked her straight on, tried to think what he could say. "I wasn't going to steal it," he said. "I came in to look at that book that's in the window—the one that's about astronauts." But his voice was shaking. He cleared his throat. "I want to buy it."

"Fine. Show me your money and I'll sell you a copy."

Hadi's attempt to save face had only ended up embarrassing him all the more. And yet he tried again. "I don't have enough money today. But when I save enough, I'll come back and buy it. How much does it cost?"

"Quit lying. You don't know how to read. You've never been to school. The only thing you understand is begging and stealing. Do you have any idea how tired we are of you people coming into our country by the millions and then expecting us to provide for you?" She pointed to the door. "Get out of here, right now."

Hadi wanted to say, *I don't steal*. He tried to say it. But all this—the embarrassment, the ugly accusations—was too much for him. "I don't . . . ," he began, but his voice broke. He stopped so he wouldn't cry. But when he squeezed his eyes shut, tears ran down his face. He gave up saying anything and hurried toward the door.

But the woman stepped from behind the counter and cut him off. She stood in front of him. He thought she might slap him, or maybe call the police. He stopped, ducked his head, wiped away the tears on his cheeks—but he didn't look at her. He wished that he had never walked into this store.

Silence continued for a long time, and Hadi didn't know whether she would let him walk around her. Finally, he looked up and saw that her face had changed. Maybe she felt sorry for him now that she had seen his tears, but he didn't want that. He was all the more humiliated.

"Am I wrong? Can you read?" she asked.

Hadi wanted to lie, but that was what she had called him, a liar, so he said instead, "Not very well. But I'm trying to learn."

"Do you go to school?"

"No. But I want to go."

"Do you like books?"

"Yes. When I was little, my father read to me. Sometimes about astronauts."

Again there was silence. Hadi decided she wouldn't stop him if he tried to leave. But he took only one step before she said, "I'm sorry. I believe you. I think you really do want to read."

Hadi looked up again. He could see in her eyes, even through her glasses, that she actually was sorry.

"I shouldn't have said those things to you. But we get frustrated here in Beirut. I don't know if you can understand that."

But Hadi *didn't* understand. He and his father only wanted to bring home enough money to provide food for their family and to pay their rent. Charities did give them clothing, and sometimes a little food, but Hadi never begged for those things. And he paid for the fruit that Garo gave him—at least a little.

"What's your name?"

"Hadi."

"Some Syrian children do go to our schools."

"I know."

"But your father sends you out to beg in the street all day."

"No. We both sell things." He pulled a package of gum from his jacket pocket. "I sell chewing gum."

She nodded, waited, seemed to think. Finally, she said, "I'd like to buy some of your gum. Can I pay you with a book?"

"No. A book costs too much. People only pay me one thousand for my gum, or maybe five hundred."

"I have an old book that's worn out and isn't worth much, but it might help you learn to read. Would you trade me a package of gum for that book?"

Hadi tried to think whether he felt all right about that. But he wanted a book, needed one. So he said, "Yes."

The woman walked back to her counter, reached underneath, and pulled out a book that looked as though it had been left out in the rain. It had a hard gray cover, no pictures on the front. "This is a book written by a Lebanese man named Kahlil Gibran. Have you heard of him?"

"No."

"He talks about life and how we should live it. He offers ways to think about the world—new ways. I've read the book many times, as you can see. But I want you to have it."

"Thank you." Hadi held the gum out to her.

The woman smiled as she took the box. He knew she didn't really want it. But he was excited to have a book of his own. He opened it, looked through some of the pages.

He saw a few words—little ones—that he knew, but most of it looked difficult.

"How will you learn to read it?"

"I have a friend who will help me. And my father. He knows how to read."

"If you want, you could stop by here, and I could help you a little."

"Thank you." But Hadi knew he wouldn't come back, at least not for now. She had already told him what she thought of him. What he wanted was to learn to read and then somehow earn enough money and come back to her store to buy the book about the astronauts.

"This is a hard book," the woman said. "You will struggle to read it at first. The words are difficult, but the meaning is deeper than the words. You can read it a hundred times in your life and still learn more each time."

Hadi really didn't understand what she meant, but he said, "*Chokran.*" He told himself, someday he would stop at this store and read the book aloud to her. He would have better clothes by then, and a job. He and Malek would figure out a way to get off the street and do things the woman could never imagine.

But for now he had a book, and he had not expected such a thing to happen. As his father had said to him, *Inshallah.*

6

As Hadi walked toward his corner, he wondered whether his eyes were red. He didn't want Malek to see him that way. But from across the intersection, Hadi could see that Malek wasn't there yet, and Hadi wondered why. He worried what might have happened to him, what Kamal might have done.

Hadi stopped at the cabstand to pick up his gum. When Rashid saw Hadi coming, he grinned. "I didn't think you would be back today," he said.

"Why?"

"I saw the man who works for Kamal watching you."

"You know Kamal?"

Rashid laughed. "Yes, I know him. I know all about him. And I know the men who work for him. You better be careful, Hadi. Don't cross Kamal or his gang. You won't get away with it."

"I know that," Hadi said, but he didn't want to say more than that. Rashid was a moody guy, and he could be pretty scary himself. Once he had told Hadi that he ought to work from the cabstand, just for a change, but then, when Hadi said he liked the other side of the street better, he had cursed him for saying so.

Hadi got his gum and crossed to the north side of the street. He decided that he might as well work from that side until Malek showed up. He could then chat with him for a minute before he returned across the street. Hadi was nervous about Malek not being there, and Rashid's assessment of Kamal had frightened him. He had been trying to tell himself that Kamal was no real threat, but Rashid knew the streets, and he obviously knew plenty about Kamal and his gang.

But things started well. Hadi felt lucky when he saw people he knew, people who always bought gum from him. In half an hour he had taken in four thousand Lebanese pounds, and then his friends, the foreigners, came by. They smiled at him, gave him two thousand pounds, and wished him a great day.

Hadi thanked them, blessed them. But as they began to drive away, he noticed something, and he ran after them. They had moved up a little and then been caught in the traffic and stopped again. He caught up to them and said, "Your tire, in back, it's low."

The man looked at Hadi curiously. Clearly he hadn't understood.

"Your tire, back here." He pointed to the tire. "It needs

air." He pressed his hands together, to show him what he meant, that the tire was going flat.

"Ah, I understand. Thank you." They both laughed, pleased that they had found a way to make sense of Hadi's gestures. The man said something else, and Hadi thought maybe it was that he would get the tire fixed, but he wasn't sure. But then the man said, "You are good friend to us, Hadi."

Hadi laughed and thanked him again, but he was surprised the man had called him a friend. They had been kind to him, but he didn't know their names or where they were from. He thought they spoke French, but he wasn't even sure of that.

But cars were honking now. The couple had to move on.

After the early traffic congestion calmed a little, Samir, the policeman who tried to keep the traffic under control, walked over to the corner and greeted Hadi. "*Marhaba,*" he said. "*Kifak?*"

"I'm very well. *Chokran.*"

But Samir wasn't just passing time. Hadi could see that in the serious way he was looking at him. Samir was a thin man, a little taller than average. He had a quiet voice even though he sometimes had to shout and blow his whistle at people. He had told Hadi once that it was a hopeless task to bring order to the streets of Beirut—but at least he had a job.

"Where's the new boy?" Samir asked.

"I don't know. I thought he would be here."

Samir nodded, looked serious. "Hadi, be careful," he said. "You're being watched."

"Now?"

"No. But I've seen people from Kamal's gang."

"Rashid said the same thing to me. Have you been talking to Rashid, or—"

"No, Hadi. I know these people; so does Rashid. When Kamal first moved into this part of town—a few months back—a street boy stood up to him. Kamal took the boy into an alley and beat him almost to death. We knew he did it, so we arrested him, but he was out of jail that same day. He has connections to people in the crime world. Those people won't be denied. They'll kill a boy like you just to prove they're in charge."

Hadi drew in some breath. He had been trying to tell himself that Kamal was just some thug who tried to scare people.

"You're a good kid, Hadi. You're respectful to people. You don't get in the way of cars or cause me any trouble. But you know that selling things on the street, the way you do, is actually illegal. If I find out our police department is making a sweep to get all you children off the street, I'll warn you ahead of time. But Kamal is a different matter. I know you need money for your family, but you won't help anyone if you get yourself killed."

Hadi nodded again. "*Chokran*. I'll be careful."

"And, Hadi, don't trust Rashid. He's a bad man too. Even worse than Kamal."

"Okay." But Hadi had a hard time believing that. Rashid had a dirty mouth, but he was just a cabdriver. It didn't seem like he would hurt anyone.

Samir walked away and Hadi tried to think what he should do. He knew with all these warnings, Baba would say he should leave now and look for a new corner. But one reason to stay was that Samir would look out for him.

It was another twenty minutes or so before Malek showed up. "How's it going?" Malek asked, as though it were a normal day. But Hadi could see that he was upset.

"What's happened?" Hadi asked.

"I didn't wake up on time. My father usually wakes me and my brothers, but he didn't do it this morning. I don't know why. But then Kamal spotted us leaving the house late. He told my brothers to hurry and get to the street, but he pulled me aside and told me I was getting no more chances. I had to start selling more tissues. And he said that you have to leave. *Today.*"

Hadi had been apprehensive for a long time now, but these words sank deep. He felt a kind of shakiness fill up his whole body. He thought maybe he should walk to Dora, talk to Baba, get his advice. But as soon as he thought of that, he knew they would have to spend the day looking for another intersection, and that meant going back to their apartment that night and telling Mama that she had to keep living with her pain. Maybe it even meant not being able to pay the rent and ending up on the street. "What if I work across the street, the way we talked about?" he asked Malek. "Did Kamal say anything about that?"

"No. I just told him I'd make you leave."

Hadi knew he was taking a huge chance—actually putting his life in danger—but why should Kamal care if he worked with cars that were going a different direction? "I'm going to work over by the cabstand. If Kamal tells you I can't do that, I'll look for a new corner, but for today I'll stay at this intersection."

"I'm sorry you have to do that, Hadi. But if I do better over here, maybe I could share some of what I make."

"Malek, no. You've got to make more just to keep Kamal satisfied. None of this is your fault. Don't worry about it." Hadi tried to sound calm, but he was still shaking.

"We can still talk sometimes," Malek said. "Come over once in a while and we'll hide behind the wall."

A wall of concrete blocks ran along the sidewalk behind the place where the boys always waited, but in one place it had broken apart and fallen down. There was space to slip through. Hadi knew they couldn't disappear for more than a minute or two at a time, but it was something.

Hadi scanned all the corners of the intersection. He couldn't see anyone who looked suspicious. "Let's hide behind the wall for a minute now. I have something to show you." He walked through the opening, and Malek followed him. Hadi had hidden his book back there. "I have a book now," he said, but he didn't tell Malek about the woman in the store and the things she had said to him.

"Can you read it?" Malek asked.

"Not really. But I figured out the name of it. It's called *The Prophet*. A man from Lebanon wrote it. It's his ideas about life—or something like that."

Malek took the book from Hadi and thumbed through it, then stopped and looked at a page. "Here's one of his ideas," he said. He read: "'Then said a rich man, Speak to us of Giving. And he answered. You give but little when you give of your possessions. It is when you give of yourself that you truly give.'"

"Do you understand what he means?" Hadi asked.

"Sure I do. If you do something for someone, that's giving of yourself."

Hadi wasn't sure that was the meaning—at least the full meaning. He had to think more about it.

Malek was saying, "This is a hard book to understand, Hadi. But you can learn lots of words from it. And your father can help you at night when you get home. Once you can read this, you'll be able to read anything."

Hadi liked hearing that. But he wondered how long it would take him to work his way through the whole book. What he was thinking now, though, was that they couldn't hide behind this wall any longer. The two had already spent too much time away from the cars. "We need to get to work," he told Malek.

"I know. And I've got to have a good day, somehow."

When they stepped through the opening, Hadi saw a man walking down the sidewalk toward them. Hadi saw him almost every day at the garbage pile. There was a dumpster halfway up the hill from the corner, and people brought their garbage there. They brought so much that the dumpster couldn't hold it all, and it spilled out into the street. This man showed up there every day.

"That's the man in black," Hadi said to Malek. "That's what I call him. He sorts through the garbage up the street."

Hadi had never said anything to the man, but Malek surprised him by smiling and saying, "*Ahlan wa sahlan.*"

The man stopped. He stared at Malek for a moment, and then he said, "Don't mock me."

"I would never do that," Malek said. "I wish you a good day."

"Why do you laugh at me?"

"I wasn't laughing. I was smiling. And I greeted you."

"See this," the man said. He pointed to a canvas bag he carried on his back. "It's full of good things that people throw away. I pull them out and give them another life. So don't mock me. I know you think I'm dirty, but someone needs to do what I do."

Hadi heard the man's Syrian accent. He had always assumed the man was a refugee like himself, but he had never known for sure. He wore black pants and a heavy black shirt. His shoulders were humped, maybe from bending over all day, but his hair was cut short, and in spite of what he did, he wasn't all that dirty—except for his hands and the heavy boots he wore.

"I think you're right," Malek said. "People do throw too many things away."

"They throw good food away, and I eat it. Sometimes it's spoiled a little, but I eat the good parts. What do you think of that?" The man glared at Malek, seeming to dare him to say that something was wrong with what he did.

"That doesn't bother me," Malek said. "You look healthy."

The man had distant eyes, as though he didn't quite see Malek even though he looked in his direction. "I am healthy," he said. "But you're mocking me."

"No, not at all. What's your name? I'll be here on this corner from now on. We should be friends."

The man took at least five seconds to respond. He continued to stare toward Malek, and then he finally said, "Amir. That's who I am." He turned his attention to Hadi. "I have a name," he said. "You didn't think so, did you?"

Hadi didn't know what to say. He didn't answer. The man—Amir—was right. Hadi hadn't thought of him as anything but the man in black who dug things from the garbage.

Malek reached out his hand and said, "It's nice to know you, Amir."

They shook hands and Amir looked at Hadi, who hesitated for a moment but then reached his hand out too. Amir said, "My hands are dirty."

Hadi nodded and said, "That's all right." And he and Amir shook hands.

When Amir was gone, Hadi was still trying to understand what had happened, but he told Malek, "That was good what you did. I never knew what his name was."

"I like to meet people," Malek said.

"But I never thought of him that way. I mean, that he had a name."

"Well, we're the boys who bother people all day, trying to sell them gum and tissues. People don't want to know our names either."

"I know."

"I have an idea about what I'd like to do in my life," Malek said. "I want to have enough money to live in a nice house. But then I'd like to help people like Amir. And people like us—the way we are now."

Hadi had spent the last two years thinking about one day at a time, nothing beyond. But Malek's words sounded right.

Hadi walked across the street, avoided Rashid as much as he could, and tried to sell his gum to the drivers who were heading north or were turning to drive up the hill to the east. Rashid stepped up next to him eventually and said, "You made a good choice. You'll do better over here."

Hadi didn't answer. He didn't know why Samir considered Rashid a bad person, but he decided to stay away from him as much as he could.

As the day went on, Hadi began to see people he

normally saw in the morning, people who probably lived in the high-rise apartment buildings on the hillside. They seemed surprised to see him in this new place, but some of them bought his gum. One woman even said, "I'm sorry you have to do this," and then gave him two thousand pounds. As it turned out, he had a very good day—better than he had ever hoped for. He had sixteen thousand lira in his pocket as the day was drawing to a close.

And then, just as he was about to quit for the day, a man did something that had happened to him only once or twice before. A young man in a nice car opened his window and asked, "Do you really take your money home to your family?"

"Yes, sir," Hadi said. "I honestly do."

"Then take this. I wish your family well." He handed Hadi a five-thousand-pound note.

Hadi was astounded. He thanked the man sincerely, and at the same time, tried to think what this all meant. This was the best day he had had in many months, and maybe now his mother could see a dentist. When he walked back across the street to join Malek for their walk home, he was feeling light. But poor Malek looked worried.

"How did it go?" Hadi asked.

"Not well enough to satisfy Kamal."

"Will he hurt you?"

"I don't know."

Hadi suddenly knew what he had to do, but he wasn't sure he could. He needed the money too. His mother did.

But he saw the fear in Malek's eyes. Besides, if Malek was in trouble, so was he. If Malek didn't do well, Kamal might be angry that Hadi was still at the intersection. Hadi reached into his pocket for his money. "Just a little while ago, a man gave me five thousand pounds," he said.

"Five thousand?"

"Yes. But I had a good day without it. You take it, and pay me back as soon as you can." He held out the bill to Malek.

"No, Hadi. I can't do that."

"It's what we agreed to—that we'll help each other. And I don't want to see your handsome face all smashed in."

Malek didn't smile, didn't reach out for the money. But when Hadi pushed the money into Malek's jacket pocket, he didn't hand it back. He said, "Thank you, Hadi. I can't believe you would do this for me."

Hadi hardly believed it himself, and already he wondered whether he had been fair to Mama. He told himself this was a good place to work, that he might do well every day. And he told himself that he was protecting himself when he helped Malek. But he also wondered: maybe he had given Malek more than money. He felt as though he had reached inside and given some of himself.

7

Hadi walked with Malek to Bourj Hammoud, and along the way Malek pointed to some simple words in Hadi's book, then helped him decipher them. Hadi was pleased with himself that he did quite well. And he appreciated Malek saying, "I'll help you every day if I can. I won't forget how much you helped me today."

So Hadi now had a book and he had Malek to help him read it. Still, hope was frightening. It was so easy to crush. Right now things could end up going worse than ever. Kamal might put a stop to this new arrangement—his working across the street—and then what would happen?

Before they reached Malek's street, the boys separated and said goodbye—just to be sure Kamal didn't see them together. As Hadi walked on to the Dora intersection with sixteen thousand Lebanese pounds in his pocket, he was glad he'd had a good day in spite of moving across the street. He decided he would not tell Baba about the other five thousand. That would be too hard to explain.

Hadi stopped to see Garo again, and he bought some vegetables and a bag of oranges—enough to hand out a whole orange to each of his siblings, and his parents, too.

But things didn't go as well at home that night as Hadi had hoped. Baba waited until the children calmed a little, and then he said, "Hadi did very well today, and I did better than yesterday, but I still don't have enough for the rent that's coming up. We'll have to get by without buying much food for another few days—maybe a week. Hadi bought some good things to eat, and mostly we'll have to depend on that."

Khaled and his sisters were too busy with their oranges to pay any attention to what Baba had said. Hadi knelt by little Aram and peeled his orange for him. Aram was hopping, grinning, as Hadi handed him the sections one at a time. He stuffed them in his mouth, too fast, and juice ran down his chin.

Hadi had known that they still needed money for rent, but he had hoped they could buy more groceries than they had lately. Sometimes Hadi wondered why Baba never told him how much money they still needed, but it wasn't his way to do that. Mama had told Hadi that Syrian men didn't discuss such things with women or children. It was always a man's place to make decisions, and especially, to handle family finances.

Baba had spoken in a kindly voice. Hadi knew how much

he hated to disappoint Mama. She was sitting in her chair, holding little Jawdat, nursing him while she covered herself with a shawl. She only nodded, didn't say a word, didn't show any disappointment, but he saw in her eyes that she was frustrated, maybe even angry.

"We'll make more money when the weather gets better. It always goes that way," Baba said. He waited, but again Mama didn't respond. Baba looked at the children and then back to Mama. "What food do we need most? I can buy a few things."

Mama looked up. Hadi could see that her anger was boiling up to the surface. "*Everything!*" she said. And then, in a voice that was splitting into a scream, "*Everything! That's what we need.* How can you ask me such a question?"

Baba looked devastated. "I know. I'm sorry."

Mama glared at him for a few seconds, and then she hung her head, kept it down a long time, and when she finally looked up, said, "It's all right. You can't help it. I shouldn't say such things. We need bread. If we have to, we can live on bread and the things Hadi brings home."

"All right. And maybe one of these days I can buy some chicken." He waited as though he wanted her to say something positive, or appreciative, but she only looked down again, so he put his coat back on and got ready to go.

When Baba left to buy the bread, Hadi sat down by his mother. "Look what I have," he said. He showed her the book.

She looked at it, but she didn't say anything.

"A woman in a bookstore gave it to me for just one package of gum. I'm going to learn to read it."

She nodded.

Hadi opened the book. He turned the pages until he found the chapter called "On Love." He had tried to read it on the bus, and Baba had helped him with some of the words. He pointed to a word and said, "That says 'love.'"

"Yes," she said. "I know that word."

"We can learn five words every day. Or more, if you want."

"Thank you, Hadi, but I can't do it. Not now. I can't think clearly."

"Because of your pain?"

She seemed hesitant to admit that that was the reason, but finally she nodded, and her eyes filled with tears. She gripped his hand, still holding Jawdat in her other arm. "I can manage a little longer," she said. "Or much longer, if that's what Allah wills for me."

But that couldn't be. Allah couldn't will such pain on Mama. No, Allah had provided her a gift and Hadi was sorry now that he had given it away. He felt almost sure Allah had intended the money for Mama—and Hadi had turned his back on her. Somehow he had to make up for that.

The next day was Friday, when Muslims gather for Jamaa prayer. But Hadi and his father worked on their corners, didn't go to mosque. Almost as though Allah was not happy with them, the rains came back and they both had slow days, with little income. Saturday was just as bad, and Hadi could see in his father's face, his movements, that he was worried all day on Sunday, the day they didn't go to the streets. Bauchrieh was mostly Christian, and Sunday was Sabbath for them. Not many cars were on the streets.

When Hadi reached his intersection on Monday morning, Malek was already there. Rain had fallen during the night and the intersection was puddled with water, but the sun was out now. Hadi was glad to see Malek, although he only waved from across the street.

There were three days left in February, and Baba was saying that they had to have at least a couple more good days if they were going to make their rent payment. The landlord had let him pay a day or two late before, but this time the disgusting little man with eyebrows the size of bird's nests had warned Baba that he wouldn't allow it again. He even claimed that he had a list of people who had offered him more for the room if Baba couldn't come up with his payment.

So Hadi felt something close to panic. He had to have a good day. And, of course, he still worried about Kamal. Every few minutes, he surveyed the area, searching for someone who might be watching him.

"Good morning, Hadi," someone said. Hadi looked around to see Rashid. Hadi had continued to avoid Rashid as best he could, but the man was friendlier than any of the other cabbies. He was younger than the others, maybe thirty or so. He was mostly bald, and what hair he had was cut short. His beard was a similar length, as though he ran clippers over his face and head, all at the same time.

"How is it working out, to sell your gum on this side of the street?" Rashid asked.

"Not bad. About the same as the other side."

"See? I told you that a long time ago. Maybe you'll do even better after more of the drivers see you here for a while. Sometimes some of us in the cabstand have an errand we like to have someone do for us. And we pay for that. Would you like to do that, if we paid you?"

"Not really. I need to stay with the cars and not go running around."

"On a slow day, we might be able to make things better for you."

Hadi didn't respond. The man sounded a little too friendly, and that made Hadi uncomfortable. The cars on the street had stopped for the light, and he went back to them, and as so often happened, he sold nothing.

When cars were moving on Malek's side, that meant the ones on Hadi's side, heading north, were stopped, so Hadi could watch what was happening. Malek no longer begged people to buy his tissues, but he did say something— words Hadi couldn't hear—and he smiled at the drivers. Hadi had always thought it was better to look more needful than happy, but he liked watching Malek, and he noticed that he was selling more tissues than he had in the beginning.

Later in the morning Hadi saw the little blue car come down the hill—the one that the foreigners drove—and he saw them buy a package of tissues from Malek, or at least give him some money. He noticed, too, that they must have asked about Hadi, because Malek turned and pointed to him. That was the worst moment of the morning. Hadi was glad they helped Malek, but he missed seeing them, talking to them for a few moments. And, of course, he missed receiving the money they would have given him.

It was almost noon when Rashid said, "Hey, Hadi, I want you to do something for me."

Hadi turned from the street and looked at Rashid.

"Come here. I need you to walk over to the Charcoutier and buy me some cigarettes."

Hadi stood his ground. These cabbies couldn't start ordering him around.

"Come on. I'll pay you two thousand lira."

That was different. "Okay," Hadi said, and he walked to Rashid, who held out some money to him and told him what brand of cigarettes he wanted. By then, however, another cabbie, Fawzi—a man with a bulging stomach and big, fat hands—said to Hadi, "I need something too. On your way back, buy me a shawarma sandwich, and you can get one for yourself."

That was even better, so Hadi took the money and

crossed the street to the west and then to the north, and he walked down the angled street to the Charcoutier. It was a big supermarket with a dazzle of food and lots of customers. The checker wasn't supposed to sell him cigarettes at his age, but she didn't seem to care.

On his way back, Hadi stopped at the chicken restaurant and ordered the shawarma sandwiches. He watched the man slice off the chicken parts that were packed onto a tall spit turning in front of a bright-red burner. The cook gathered up the meat he had sliced and dropped it onto rounds of flat bread, then tossed in French fries, pickles, and a thick white garlic sauce. Hadi loved the smell of the chicken and the spices. He could taste the sandwich already.

Hadi paid the six thousand pounds, then walked back to the cabstand, where Rashid took the cigarettes and handed over two thousand lira from the change. Fawzi took the bag, pulled out one of the sandwiches, then, surprisingly, also handed Hadi two thousand lira. He grinned, showing a missing tooth.

"No, it's okay," Hadi said. "You bought me a sandwich."

"That's all right. You work hard all day. We watch you. This gives you a little more to take home today."

Hadi didn't argue. But he did wonder again what was going on. The cabbies had never treated him so well. Still, they had given him four thousand pounds he hadn't expected, and it made a big difference. He thought maybe this wouldn't be such a bad place to work after all. He looked across the street and saw Malek, who had surely seen him cross over with the sandwiches. Hadi sat down on the bench, where the cabbies always sat, ripped open the paper, and took a bite of the shawarma. It was still hot, and it tasted wonderful. But Hadi ate what he thought was half, and then he walked across the street. "Do you want to eat the rest of this?" he asked.

"Sure I do."

Hadi handed the sandwich to Malek, and the boys walked behind the wall. "Are you selling much today?" Hadi asked.

"Some," he said.

But Hadi heard some discouragement in Malek's voice. Hadi was pretty sure that Malek didn't like working alone either—even if he smiled at people.

Malek ate the sandwich in about six big bites, and Hadi knew he was hurrying to get back to work. All the same, he asked, "Do you have your book with you?"

"Sure. It's right here." He patted his middle.

"Let me teach you a few words."

"There's a chapter about love," Hadi said. "I tried to read it last night, but I don't understand what it says." He turned the pages until he found the chapter, then handed the book to Malek.

Malek read for a time. "This isn't about having a girl-friend. It's about loving everyone. Try to read this sentence."

Hadi pronounced the sound of the letters and recognized the first word: "when." And he knew the word "love." But he didn't know the next word, and Malek struggled with it too.

"It's 'beckon,'" Malek said. "I think that means to go like this." He waved his hand toward himself. "You know, like to call someone to you."

Hadi was able to decipher the other words after that: "When love beckons you, follow him."

"Right," Malek said. "Do you see what that means?"

"No."

"I think it's like, if love calls to you, go where it leads you."

"But where does it lead me?"

"To love people, I guess. I'd have to read this all the way through to figure it out."

Hadi tried to think whether he loved people. He remembered the way Malek had treated Amir. Since then he had greeted the man every time he had seen him. He liked that. But he wasn't sure he loved Amir. And the foreign couple. He appreciated what they did for him, but he doubted that he loved them. The same with Garo. It didn't seem possible that a person could just love everyone.

"I like this book," Malek said. "I'd like to read it all the way through sometime."

"Okay. Maybe we can take turns."

"But you keep it for now. So you can practice every day. You're learning really fast." He glanced toward the opening in the wall. "But you better not stay here too long. We need to get back to work."

Hadi smiled. "It's time to go love all these people in the cars," he said.

"I think I only love the ones who give me money," Malek said. "I'll get around to the others later."

The boys grinned at each other, and then Hadi put his book back inside his jacket and walked across the street. He didn't sell as much gum as he would have liked in the afternoon, but then the foreign couple came by on his side of the street, and they stopped even though the light was green. Hadi stood on the passenger side of the car while people honked and tried to get around the car. The woman gave him two thousand pounds. He was happy to know that they would still look for him on this side of the street.

But he had been waiting to ask them a question. "What are your names?"

Both laughed, and the woman said, "I told you once, but maybe you didn't understand me. Riser is our name. Emil and Klara Riser. Can you say it?"

"Riser." He knew he sounded different when he said it, but they told him he was right. "Where do you live? I mean, when you're not here?"

"Switzerland. In the mountains."

Hadi had heard of this country, but he knew nothing about it.

"We speak French at home."

"*Merci*," Hadi said, and he laughed, as did they. He thought of what he might say to them, and finally came up with, "I like you."

"Yes. We are friends, Hadi. We like you, too."

Hadi could think only of what Malek had done. He reached through the window and extended his hand to them. They both shook his hand while drivers continued to honk and complain.

After the Risers turned right at the corner and drove up the hill, Rashid walked over to him.

"Who are those people?" he asked. "I notice they stop and buy your gum every time they see you. Why do they do that?"

Hadi shrugged.

"Come here a minute," Rashid said. "There's something I want to talk to you about." Hadi didn't like the sound of this.

Rashid sat down on the bench and waited for Hadi to sit next to him. But Hadi remained standing, and he said, "I need to keep working the cars."

"How much do you make each day?"

"It's different every day."

"Maybe ten thousand lira on a good day?"

"Sometimes." Baba always told him not to tell anyone how much money he took in.

"There are better ways to make money, Hadi."

"I don't want to do anything else."

"I'm not talking about one or two thousand pounds. I'm talking about a lot more."

"No. What I make is okay," Hadi said. He turned to walk away.

"Wait a minute, Hadi. We're friends. I want to help

you out. I have some simple errands you could do for me sometimes—sort of like today, going to get cigarettes for me. But I can pay you very well."

"No. My father wants me to sell gum and not . . . do anything else."

Hadi walked back to the street, but as he did, Rashid said, "Think about it, Hadi. You could feed your family, make things better for them. I just want to help you out."

Baba had warned Hadi about men who made offers that didn't sound right, and Samir had told him to stay away from Rashid. What he felt certain of was that the Risers were his friends. And so was Garo. Maybe that was the same thing as saying that he loved them. But Rashid only *said* he was a friend. Hadi didn't trust the man.

8

Hadi's income for the day was not great, but the extra four thousand had helped. When he handed over twelve thousand pounds that night, Baba said, "Not quite as good as you did yesterday."

"I know," Hadi said. "But it's been a lot worse at times. And I got more food from Garo than usual. I helped him move a box this morning, and he said he owed me something extra."

Baba nodded. "That's good, and we have two more days. We should have enough, but nothing extra. What exactly did you bring from Garo?"

Hadi held up his net. "Potatoes," he said. "Lots of them. And carrots, leeks, cabbage, and two tomatoes. We can make a big soup. Everyone will like that."

"That's good, Hadi. You did well. Once I pay the rent, we can stock up on a few groceries before we start saving for next month. But the electricity bill is coming up before long, and more than anything, we need to get your mother to a dentist."

Baba looked serious but not quite so worried as he had been lately. At least it appeared they were going to get by again. But Hadi wondered whether he would have even worse days in the future. What about days when the cabbies didn't send him on errands? He had hoped that this new side of the street might actually turn out better, but now it seemed it would only be more unpredictable.

Maybe Baba sensed Hadi's concern. He said, "On the bus, let's look at your book. I'll help you learn some words tonight."

Hadi was happy to hear him say that. Hadi had not wanted to bother him. But when they sat together on the bus, Baba told him to pick a passage and try to read it.

Hadi turned to the chapter on love again. He pointed to a word and asked his father what it was.

"Desire," his father said. "You know—something you want."

"I 'desire' to eat tabbouleh, not potatoes and bread," Hadi said.

Baba laughed. "Yes. Exactly. See, you do know that word."

"And what's this one?"

"'Fulfill.' That's something you complete, or you accomplish what someone asks of you."

Hadi read slowly, "'Love has no other *desire* but to *fulfill* itself.' What does that mean?"

"Hadi, I know this book, *The Prophet*. It's what we call 'philosophical.' Many of the ideas are hard for anyone to comprehend. Gibran is talking about love as though it has a will of its own. It's something we'll both have to think about. But I wish you had a simpler book to learn from."

"I know. But I can learn new words from it. I need to know *all* words."

"No one knows every word."

That surprised Hadi. He thought that people who went to school learned all the words in every book. He at least wanted to know each word in this book. So he and Baba worked their way through the whole page, and Hadi was relieved to know that once he could pronounce the words, he usually knew their meaning.

"Hadi," Baba finally said, "you're very smart. Do you know that? I'm sorry you've had to spend your days on the street, not in school."

Hadi knew that it hurt Baba to keep him out of school. But Hadi didn't want to make him feel any worse, so he said nothing more. He looked out the window. He saw run-down buildings, which were now making a silhouette like a picket fence. People on the street were moving about, sometimes walking through the slow traffic. In a neighborhood like this, lots of the people were Syrians—people like him who tried each day to earn enough to feed their families.

They were "displaced," or at least that was what people in government offices called them. When Hadi had been nine or ten, he had gone with his father to apply for "legal status." He hadn't understood what that meant exactly, but he knew his family needed certain kinds of papers or they would get in trouble. The man in the office had sounded unfriendly, impatient. He had asked Baba if he and his family were "temporarily displaced," and Baba had said yes. Afterward, Hadi had asked what the man had meant, and Baba said, "We had to leave Syria and find a new place to live. Now we're 'displaced'—forced to live away from our home."

"You mean we're in the wrong place?"

"Not exactly. We're where we have to be for now, but it's not our home."

"But that man, when he said, 'displaced,' it sounded like he thought something was wrong with us."

"I know. That's why we have to be good people, so the Lebanese won't have any reason to dislike us."

Hadi wondered about that now. He never said bad things to the drivers in the cars. He thanked people and blessed them when they bought his chewing gum. He did as Baba and Samir told him, didn't cause problems, but lots of people hated him anyway. Baba always told him not to hate the people back, but he didn't know how to change the way he felt when someone called him names.

But there were worse things. Hadi thought of little Marwa back in Aleppo, her dusty body, her legs twisted the wrong way. And he thought of a man he had seen, gasping for air, then vomiting on the street. Someone told him that the man had breathed chlorine gas. He hadn't known what that was, still didn't; he only knew that people killed each other, and not always with bombs. He doubted he could love the people who'd killed Marwa. He didn't even want to try. So he did what he always tried to do: force all those memories out of his mind.

Hadi made the soup that night, with Mama's guidance, and then he sat in a corner with Khaled and tried to help him read some of the words in the book. He knew Khaled needed to learn to read too. But Khaled didn't last long. "I don't like to do this," he said.

"Don't you want to learn to read?" Hadi asked him.

"Not tonight" was all he said.

Little Aram had climbed onto Hadi's lap. He liked to have Hadi home, liked to wrestle with him or get tossed about, or just to cuddle next to him when he was cold. Across the room, Aliya, Rabia, and Samira had been playing with dolls—rag dolls they had received from the same charity that gave them clothing. But holding the dolls, pretending to feed them, had apparently lost interest for them. They were laughing now and using the dolls as weapons, swinging them and hitting each other. Hadi hated to see them do that.

Mama had been cleaning up after dinner, but now she turned and looked at the girls. "Please don't," she said. "I'll take those dolls if you don't treat them right, and I'll give them to girls who want them."

Aliya stood up and said, "That's fine with me. Here—take

mine." She tossed the doll at her mother. It fell at Mama's feet. She picked it up, stared back at Aliya, but she didn't say anything. Always before, Mama would have talked to Aliya about such behavior, punished her perhaps, maybe even gotten angry with her, but she didn't seem to have the energy now.

It was Baba who said, "You must not talk to your mother that way, Aliya. Tell her you're sorry."

"I'm *not* sorry," Aliya said. "I hate that dirty old doll." She looked at her sisters, clearly hoping they would laugh.

But this was something new. Hadi could see that Baba didn't know what to do. "Aliya," he said, "it's been a hard day. We're all tired. Let's be kind to each other."

Aliya stood with her hands still on her hips, but she didn't say anything. What Hadi understood about her was that she had always been a busy, active little girl. These winter days inside were almost more than she could stand, and misbehavior must have seemed a way to create a change from all the boredom.

Hadi got up and walked to Aliya. He put his hand softly on her shoulder. "Remember when I taught you the alphabet?" he asked.

Aliya looked surprised. "Yes."

"Do you remember how to write the letters?"

"I don't know."

"Let's learn letters tonight, okay? Khaled will help me teach you."

Baba was nodding, and Aliya, without admitting it, seemed interested, maybe happy for Hadi's attention.

Little Jawdat had begun to cry. Mama walked to the corner, where Jawdat had been sleeping on some blankets. She picked him up and then sat on her chair. She wrapped her arms around him, covered herself, and prepared to nurse him. Hadi gathered his siblings close to Mama, so she could learn too, and they worked on their letters.

What Hadi was noticing by then was that Mama's face was more swollen. She was probably relieved that Hadi had calmed the children, but she looked broken. He knew her pain was terrible. Somehow, he and Baba had to do better these next few days.

When Hadi and Baba reached the Dora intersection the following morning, Baba only said, "God bless you, Hadi." But there was more in his voice than his words, and Hadi knew that he was thinking about Mama too.

Hadi walked faster than usual to his intersection. At the cabstand, Rashid was sitting on the bench smoking a cigarette, wearing the same blue coat he had worn all winter and a black cap pulled down tight over his eyes. But he raised the cap when he saw Hadi, and he said, "Good morning, Hadi. I hope you have a successful day."

Hadi only said, "Thank you," and then asked for his gum.

Rashid opened the cabinet and brought out a carton, which he handed to Hadi. "I don't know why anyone would buy such junk," he said. "You need something better to sell."

Hadi didn't answer. He filled his jacket pockets with the various flavors, and then he walked to the curb. He got there as the cars were stopping, so he immediately cut across to the driver's side of the first car, then walked up the line, showing the little boxes to the drivers. He stopped each time, tried to make eye contact, to nod, and to plead with his eyes but not look too sad. He had to find a way to do better today.

But this technique didn't make any difference, and then rain began to fall. People kept their windows closed—and no one bought his gum.

After an hour without a sale, Hadi felt desperate. He was thinking he might try saying, "My mother needs to have a tooth pulled. She's in bad pain." It was true, after all.

As he waited on the curb, Rashid called to him, "Hadi, go get me a pack of cigarettes, will you?"

That would be something: a start. Maybe Rashid would pay him two thousand pounds again. So he hurried to the Charcoutier, bought the pack of cigarettes, then jogged back. When he handed over the cigarettes, Rashid said, "So, is this a bad morning for you? I haven't seen anyone buy your gum."

"They don't buy as much when it rains," Hadi said.

"That's too bad. The taxi business gets better when it rains."

Hadi wanted to ask him why he sat around at the cab-stand most of the time if that was the case, but he didn't. He was watching Rashid wrap the bills Hadi had brought back to him around a thick roll of money and he was starting to worry. Maybe he wasn't going to give Hadi anything today. But then he said, "I'll tell you what. You're having a bad day, so I'll pay you a little better this time." He peeled off five one-thousand-pound bills, folded them, and handed them all to Hadi.

"No. That's too much," Hadi said. "Just give me two, like before."

"Hadi, don't worry about it. I know your family needs the money. I like to help my friends when I can. And besides, you had to run to the store in the rain. You deserve more today."

Hadi almost shoved all the money back at him. He had heard a false tone in Rashid's voice. He didn't know why he had started claiming that they were friends. But five thousand, so early, meant the start of a good day, when he had seen only a bad one ahead. He couldn't turn the money down.

"*Chokran,*" Hadi said, and he bowed his head just a little.

"What about a blessing from Allah? That's what you tell those people in the cars?"

"*Allah yehmik,*" Hadi said automatically.

"No question. I'm sure he will," Rashid said, and he laughed. "I hope he looks after you, too."

Hadi knew that Rashid was making fun of his religion, and he hated that. He was tempted to give the money back, but he couldn't get himself to do it.

Fawzi was sitting on the bench, leaning back, his big stomach pushing over his belt, his shirt showing beneath his jacket. He laughed. "Allah needs to help Rashid," he said. "He's a terrible driver. Look at his taxi. It's full of dents."

"Allah needs to bless all the crazy drivers in this city," Rashid said. "They keep running into me."

"Hadi, save your blessings," Fawzi said, and he was still laughing. "Allah looks out for polite boys—not for guys like Rashid."

Hadi had heard enough. They had no right to talk that way. He went back to the street, but things did not get better. He got one sale, for one thousand, but six thousand, with the middle of the day coming on, was not good enough. He was not likely to do as well as he had the day before.

It was close to noon when Rashid walked over to Hadi. "I have a fare," he said. "I've got to be on my way. Will you do something for me while I'm gone?"

Hadi didn't like the sound of this, but he turned from the curb. "I need to keep working. I haven't made—"

"No. It's nothing like that. You can keep working. But a man is coming by. He'll stop right there at the curb. I told him to tell you, 'I hope this rain stops before we have a flood.' That's how you'll know it's him. When he says that, just hand him this." Rashid held out a small box wrapped in brown paper.

"I'd rather not. I want to—"

"It's just a simple thing. The guy who will stop here is

a friend of mine, and I have something for him. I told him to stop by here and pick it up. But now I have to leave, so I called him and told him what to say so you would know he's the right man."

Hadi could only wonder why the man in the car couldn't just say that he was Rashid's friend. It sounded like something bad was going on if they had to use secret words to make their connection. Hadi knew what his father had told him—and what Samir had said. But it was just a package, and Rashid was pushing it into his hands. It wasn't much to do, and maybe Rashid would give him a thousand or two for his trouble.

So he took it.

Rashid got into his taxi and drove away. Maybe ten minutes later, a man stopped in the line of cars, three back from the corner, and he waved for Hadi to come to his car. When Hadi approached, he rolled down the window and said, "I hope the rain stops before we have a flood."

Hadi nodded, then handed him the package. The man thanked him and handed him two thousand pounds. Hadi hadn't expected that. But the bigger surprise occurred when Rashid came back. He asked Hadi whether the man had come, and Hadi said that he had and he had delivered the package. "*Allah yehmik*," Rashid said, laughing, and then he stuffed some money into Hadi's jacket pocket. It was only after Hadi had worked his way down the line of cars that he looked to see how much money Rashid had given him.

Ten thousand pounds!

Now Hadi knew that something wasn't right. Baba had told him that cabbies were known for selling drugs. And what else, in a small package, could be worth ten thousand lira just to hand to someone? He had to give the money back.

But as he walked to the cabstand, he thought about the problems this money would solve. Hadi now had almost twenty thousand pounds in his pocket. It was the kind of day he had needed to have. And Hadi hadn't sold the package to the man; he had only passed it along to him. He didn't even know for certain what was in the package.

So he kept the money, and with a few more sales that afternoon, he had twenty-three thousand pounds.

When he stopped at Garo's stand that night, he said, "I need some vegetables, if you have them, and some fruit, too. I can pay."

"It sounds as though you had a good day," Garo said. He leaned back, smiled, his mustache bending.

"Yes, it was."

"So what's the matter? You don't look very satisfied."

"It's nothing," Hadi said. He was looking about, trying to see what vegetables he might like to take home—and trying not to look at Garo. "My mother has a bad toothache. I'm worried about her, but she'll be going to a dentist one of these days."

"Then I won't charge you anything, and I'll fill up some good bags for you."

"No. Baba says I should always pay."

"And you always do. But friends can help friends. It's what they ought to do."

Rashid had said almost the same thing. But Hadi heard the difference. Garo meant what he said.

Hadi nodded, thanked Garo, and meant the blessing that he offered him.

When he reached the Dora intersection that night, he had twenty-three thousand lira to give Baba—and three bags of vegetables and fruit.

"What happened?" Baba asked.

"It was a good day," Hadi said, "one of my best days ever."

"Even in the rain?"

"Yes, even in the rain." But he couldn't look at his father. He worried that Baba could look into his eyes and know that he was lying.

9

Hadi didn't think he should hand over any more packages for Rashid. The only problem was, Baba told him while they were on their way home that with Hadi's twenty-three thousand pounds, he had enough money to pay the rent and to take Mama to the dentist, but there wouldn't be anything left to buy the medicine Mama would need. He was sure her tooth was infected. She would need pills for the pain, but also antibiotics for the infection, and he had no idea what that would cost. "Is there any chance you'll do as well tomorrow?" Baba asked him.

"I doubt it," Hadi said. "I'll try."

"I don't mean to expect too much," Baba said. "I just wondered if this new corner will be better for you all the time now."

Hadi thought of saying that it would probably be worse. After all, most of the money had come from Rashid. But he was also thinking that he knew what it would probably take to have another good day.

When they reached home, Baba told Hadi to take five thousand lira and buy food to add to what Garo had given him. Baba would take Mama to the dentist. Hadi was relieved that he was taking her, but when they came back, Mama looked worse than before. Baba said that the tooth had broken and the dentist had had to "dig out" the root. Mama's jaw—the whole side of her face—was swollen worse than ever. She looked as though she had been beaten up. All the color was gone from her face, except around her eyes, which looked bruised. Hadi knew she had to be in worse pain than before.

Hadi felt sick to look at her. "Did you get any pills for her?" he asked.

"Yes. Enough to last two days—but she'll need more."

"I'll have a good day again tomorrow," Hadi said. "I'll make sure I do."

Baba gave him a quick glance, as though he was understanding something for the first time. "How will you do that, Hadi? What do you mean?"

"Nothing." He looked away.

Baba was watching him, looking concerned, and Hadi knew he was trying to decide whether he believed him. But finally he said, "Let's hope so. At least let's hope for one more good day." And Hadi thought he understood. Baba was terrified of the things Hadi could get himself involved in, but he also knew how serious Mama's condition was.

In the morning, when Hadi went back to the cabstand,

he didn't ask Rashid for another package to deliver. But if Rashid asked him to hand over another box, he had already decided he'd do it one more time.

But Hadi had another reason for concern. Not long after he had arrived that morning, a man wearing a black jacket— a man Hadi had seen before—appeared on the corner to the west, stopped and smoked a cigarette. He seemed to be scanning the intersection. He could certainly see that Hadi had left his usual corner and wasn't working with Malek, but Hadi had to wonder, was that good enough? If this man worked for Kamal, as Hadi suspected he did, Kamal might decide to force Hadi away from the intersection entirely, and Hadi might not make much money at all in the coming days. He had to do as well as he could today.

A storm moved in during the morning and turned into a downpour at about ten o'clock. Hadi had taken in only three thousand pounds at that point, and the cabbies had not asked him to run any errands. All morning Hadi had been watching Malek across the street. He noticed that Malek had made some sales, but the ones who were buying from Malek were mostly people who had always bought from Hadi. It was Malek's corner now. Hadi told himself to be glad his friend was doing well, not to feel any resentment. But he was beginning to feel desperate. He had to have a good day.

When the hard rain had begun, Hadi had gone to the bench where the cabbies sat. There was a narrow roof over the seating area, enough to provide a little protection, and five men had gathered there to stay dry. Hadi stayed at the end of the bench, didn't sit down next to the cabbies. He simply didn't want to get drenched.

Hadi watched the furious blast of rain fill up the streets in only a few minutes. The water was running off the hill, carrying garbage and refuse of all kinds. The rain let up in twenty minutes or so, and Hadi walked back toward the street. But every car that passed now sent up a wave of water. Hadi knew he had to get back to work, but he stayed away from the curb when the cars were moving, and that made it easy for Rashid to approach him without calling attention to himself. When he did, his words didn't surprise Hadi. "I have another friend coming by today," he said. "Would it be too much trouble for you to hand him a little package—the way you did yesterday?"

Rashid ran his fingers over his short hair, as if to wipe away raindrops, but Hadi saw that he was trying to act natural. He also saw Rashid take a look to the middle of the intersection. Was that to see whether Samir was watching? Hadi thought of the danger he was putting himself in if Samir saw him pass the package to a driver, but he had to say yes just one more time. "I could do that," he said.

"Good. And you understand. I'll pay you the same each time."

Hadi felt his breath catch. Now Rashid was saying that they were entering into business together, that they were striking a deal. "Okay," he said, "I can do it again today—as a favor."

"It's not a favor, Hadi. I'm paying you. You understand that, don't you?"

Hadi knew he had to say no, not agree to some sort of arrangement, but he also had to have another good day. For his mother. "Yes," Hadi said. "I understand."

Hadi took the package and Rashid drove away in his taxi. In a few minutes, a man in a fancy black BMW stopped at the curb, leaned across the front seat, and said, "I hope this rain stops before we have a flood."

"I think we have one already," Hadi said. He smiled, but he was feeling the wet and the cold. The flood.

The man laughed, but he glanced toward the intersection, as though checking to see if he was being watched. When he reached out, Hadi saw a huge ring on his finger—gold with stones, maybe diamonds. He took the package and said, "Wait. Let me give you this." And this time it was ten thousand pounds. Hadi was stunned.

When Rashid returned, Hadi got his other ten thousand. He felt great relief, even appreciation, but as he returned to selling gum, he also felt deeply ashamed. He was sure he had enough money now to pay for the pills his mother needed, but he hated to imagine what she would think of him if she knew how he had earned it. Still, he told himself he wasn't a drug dealer. If he hadn't passed the boxes along, Rashid would have found someone else to do it.

Not long after that, Fawzi asked Hadi to walk to the garlic chicken restaurant and bring back shawarma sandwiches for himself and for Hadi. Hadi was glad for the food, but he was even happier when the man at the shop told him that it was three-for-the-price-of-two day. So Hadi took a sandwich back to Fawzi, accepted a tip for doing so, and then walked across the street. He smiled at Malek. "It's your lucky day," he said. "I have a shawarma for you. A whole one."

Malek grinned. "That's good," he said. "I'm hungry today."

"I'll eat mine here with you, Malek," Hadi said. "Let's go behind the wall." He felt fairly safe since the man in the black jacket was gone now.

The boys stepped through the opening in the wall and each sat down on a concrete block. The rain had started up again, not heavy yet, but the empty lot behind the wall was muddy, and trash had gathered in piles against the wall.

"I was doing well this morning, before the rain came," Malek said. "That slowed everything down."

"But you sell more than you used to, don't you?"

"Yes. Kamal even complimented me for doing better. But then he said I should do even better."

"Has he mentioned me?"

"No. Maybe he won't care now that you've crossed the street. And, Hadi, I'll pay you back the five thousand. Maybe I can give you a thousand at a time, when I have better days."

"Don't worry about it, Malek. Just do well and keep Kamal happy. I'm managing all right on the other side of the street, and I should do even better as more drivers get to know me."

"All right. But I will pay you back." Malek bit into his sandwich, chewed for a time, and then said, "This is good. Thanks for getting it for me." He slapped Hadi on the shoulder. "Hadi, you're the best friend I've ever had."

Hadi heard in Malek's voice that he meant it; he wasn't just joking the way he had when he first showed up. So Hadi told the truth: "You're the only friend I've had since I came to Beirut."

"We need to stay friends, always."

Hadi wanted that. More than anything. He needed a friend he could depend on. "Malek," he said, and he took a long breath, "did some of your friends die in Syria?"

Malek looked over at him, and Hadi thought he saw in his eyes that he was hesitant to say anything. He finally said, "When the bombs hit my town, lots of people died."

"But any close friends?"

"Two girls from my school. Sisters. I always joked with them. But I liked the older one, Yara. She was a year older than me, and she was very pretty. She didn't know I liked her."

"Do you think about her now?"

"Sure I do."

"But at night, do you have dreams about the bombs? And wake up scared?"

"No. But all our bombs came on one night. You had to hear them for a long time."

"Yes," Hadi said, "but I'm sorry she was killed." He decided not to say anything more, but he was relieved to let Malek know about his dreams. He had never told his parents.

"We have to figure things out," Malek said. "So we can stay friends, and not always . . . be stuck at this intersection."

"We *will* figure it out, Malek."

Malek nodded, but he was changing. He had sounded as though he was trying to convince himself, not Hadi.

Hadi knew that feeling, knew how terrible it was to admit to yourself that you have no choice, that what you're doing is what you have to keep doing. "I have an idea," he told Malek. "The foreign couple—their name is Riser—told me once that they could help get me into a school. The trouble was, it started at three o'clock. I couldn't leave that early. But what if we took turns leaving early? One of us could go to school for a while and then the other. And we could help each other, the way we talked about, and make sure the one who left early still took home enough money."

Malek took a long look at Hadi, as if he were considering the possibility, but then he said, "We're not making enough as it is, Hadi. How could we do that?"

Hadi didn't dare say what he was thinking: that he could keep delivering the packages for Rashid. He could finish making things right for Mama, and then he could make things right for Malek—and for himself. "We need to think about it" was what he said to Malek. "If we both start doing better in the spring, it might work."

Hadi could see that Malek was caught in between two ways of thinking. He wanted to believe in a future, but he was also beginning to see the reality that Hadi had been looking at for a long time. "I guess we can hope for something like that," Malek said. "But my father won't hear of it for now."

"Maybe, if you start to bring home—"

"We need to get back to work," Malek said. He started eating faster, taking big bites.

"We have to have a plan," Hadi said. "Getting back into school would be a start. Maybe things will change and we can find a country that will let us in, or we'll . . . I don't know. We just can't give up." It was what Malek had told him a few weeks back, and it was what Hadi wanted him to start saying again.

"All right. We'll keep hoping." But the words sounded weak.

"We can share our money. If you have bad days, let me know." But he worried how that might sound, so he added, "And I'll tell you if I need a little more at times."

"Okay," Malek said, but he didn't sound convinced.

Hadi felt good about the idea. He could start passing some of his money on to Malek and satisfy Kamal each day. It didn't seem so wrong to take money from Rashid if he used it to help other people. Maybe that was "giving of himself."

As Hadi approached the cabstand, he saw Rashid glaring at him. "Come here," Rashid said. "Where have you been?"

He didn't want to explain about the free shawarma, so he only said, "I walked over to say hello to Malek—the boy who works across the street."

"That boy is working for Kamal. Don't have anything to do with those people."

So Rashid thought he owned Hadi now. But Hadi didn't care if he did. The more he thought about it, Hadi was the one taking advantage of Rashid. He was finding a way out of his mess while he was letting Rashid think that he was scared of him.

"How is your family doing?" Rashid asked. "A little better since I've helped you out lately?"

"My mother has a bad tooth. Baba finally got her to a dentist yesterday. But she still needs medicine." Hadi knew exactly what he was saying: that he did need Rashid's help and he was willing to accept it—but he wasn't about to thank him for it.

Rashid was standing with his feet set wide apart, his arms crossed over his chest. He waited for Hadi to look at him again. "So you need the money. I understand that. But here's what you have to understand. You delivered my packages and I paid you; you're my partner now. If anything should go wrong, remember, the police don't like you little Syrian *pests* who run loose on our streets. If I ever got in trouble, so would you."

"Why would you get in trouble?"

"Don't act stupid. You know what we're doing."

"I only handed over the—"

"That's not what the police would say. And I'll tell you something else. The police are not your biggest worry. The people who give me those packages don't put up with snitches of any kind. They don't worry about slitting a few throats if that's what they have to do to protect themselves. Do you understand what I'm saying?"

Hadi didn't respond at first, but Rashid kept watching him. So Hadi nodded.

"I'm going to have more friends coming by, and when they do, I will be gone and you will hand over the packages. I'll pay you—but I won't always be so generous with my money. I feel now that I've paid you more than you deserve. So don't start thinking that you can stop being my partner. Try it and see what happens to you. Or even what might happen to that mother you're so worried about. Your whole family. You work for me now, and the only way to be safe— and keep your family safe—is to stay partners with me."

Hadi nodded again. But all his justifications seemed empty now. The only thing left was fear.

"But, Hadi, let's not talk about slitting throats. We're friends, right? And your family is doing better now that we're working together. They'll do better and better so long as we continue this way. I'm Allah, as far as you're concerned, and I'm blessing you every day. You need to thank me."

Hadi didn't say anything.

"Let's hear it. Thank me. Bless me."

Hadi didn't want to do it.

"Bless me, Hadi. Right now. Either that or take a walk with me. There are some alleys around here we may want to visit."

Hadi took his time, but finally he said, *"Allah ysallmak."*

"Thank you, Hadi. Peace is exactly what I want. You chose the right words. Let there be peace between us." He patted Hadi on the shoulder. "I know we can work together in love and peace."

10

Hadi went back to the cabstand every morning, and most days Rashid had packages for him to deliver. Some days he had two or three. But he wasn't paying Hadi as much as he had at first. He would pay him at the end of the day, and it was never the same rate. One day he would give him ten thousand lira after he passed along three packages, but another day it would be only five thousand. Once he paid him nothing and told Hadi that he didn't like his attitude, that he wasn't as friendly as he had been.

Hadi was starting to recognize the people who passed by him south to north each day, and more of them were buying gum from him. The better weather also helped. So if he picked up an extra five thousand or more from Rashid, along with a good tip from the person who accepted the package, he was reporting more good days to Baba, and Baba showed no signs that he suspected what he was doing. On days when Hadi took in too much money, he tucked some in his shoe, then brought it out on slower days. Bringing home a similar amount each day made the whole family more comfortable.

But Hadi was more on edge than ever. He was afraid he would be caught, afraid what that would mean for his family, and afraid that if he made a mistake with Rashid, his family's lives would be in danger. He also worried that Malek would see what was going on and think less of him. Samir was nearby all the time too, and Hadi feared that the man had seen him hand packages to people.

Each time he worried about his risk, though, he thought of the medicine he had been able to buy for Mama. She had recovered from her infection, and with improved weather she was taking the children outside now and then. Most important, Hadi was bringing home enough money to buy more groceries than the family had had for a long time, and that relieved Mama's biggest concern. He could see new light in her eyes these days. She talked more, laughed at times, and she was dealing better with Aliya. But Aliya was happier, too, and so were all the kids. So much of the tension everyone had felt all winter was letting up. Baba was more changed than anyone, with so much burden lifted off him.

In spite of all this, Hadi wished that he had never crossed the street, that he was still working with Malek, laughing with him, talking about the things they wanted to do some-day. He still sneaked across the street to Malek long enough to get help with a few words he couldn't figure out himself, but he could never stay more than a minute or two. Hadi's reading skills were improving fast, and he was getting additional help from his father. The electricity was going off quite often, but the sun was up longer. That made reading at home easier. And he was still thinking that if circumstances continued to improve, maybe he and Malek could start going to school, the way they had talked about.

One morning in late March, when Rashid had driven off with a fare, Hadi hurried across the street and stood next to Malek on his corner. "I wrote down some words I want you to help me with," he said, "but first I want to talk to you about something in my book."

"Okay. What's that?"

He held his book out to Malek and said, "Read this part right here. It's the part we read a long time ago. But I've been thinking more about what it might mean."

Hadi had wanted to tell Malek all the things that had been going through his head. Each night, after the electricity went off, Hadi had lots of time to think, and he often found himself wondering about the ideas he had come across. The more he read, the more he understood, and he felt that something was right about what the author was saying. Gibran thought people should live in peace and treat others with kindness. The world Hadi saw every day was hectic, the drivers at the intersection all fighting a kind of battle. And the shouting and honking he heard sounded like hatred. Hadi didn't want to live in a world like that. He didn't want anyone to hate him, and he didn't want to hate. He had found a friend in Malek, and now they rarely talked. He didn't want to give up the promises they had made to each other.

Lately, when he arrived at the intersection, if Rashid was not there yet, Hadi walked up the hill and said hello to Amir, who was usually at the garbage pile first thing in the morning. But after he greeted Amir, he walked a few paces beyond the garbage. A flower tree like one he had known in Syria was in full blossom now, brilliant pink. He just liked to look at it as often as he could. It was his best memory of Syria. He wished at times that he could go back and see if the one in Aleppo was still alive, but Hadi knew what the neighborhood would look like. It was all rubble now, and everyone was gone. Little Marwa was buried somewhere, and Mohammad and his other friends had all moved away. He liked to think that Mohammad was all right now, that he didn't think about Marwa too much. And the tree, too, that he and Baba had tried to save—he hoped it was blossoming in the spring.

Malek read the sentences Hadi was pointing to: "'You give but little when you give of your possessions. It is when you give of yourself that you truly give.'" Then he said, "Sure I remember that. What are you thinking about it?"

"Well, first of all, I don't really have any possessions."

"Sure you do. Clothes. Shoes. Your book."

"Well, yes. And I have big ears. They'll be mine forever."

"Just don't put them down somewhere and forget where you left them."

Hadi rolled his eyes, but he was glad Malek was making dumb jokes again. And with the good weather, he was making more money on his side of the street. He had told Hadi that Kamal hadn't been so harsh with him lately.

"Here's what I was thinking about last night," Hadi said. He pointed up the street. "See Amir up there sorting the garbage?"

"Sure."

"I walk up there and say hello to him almost every day. And when he sees me, he says hello, and he calls me Hadi. I shake hands with him no matter how dirty he is."

"That's good," Malek said.

"I know. But I never thought of doing that until you did it. You changed me. You gave me 'yourself.'" Hadi was embarrassed now that he had said the words, but in the dark, the night before, he had wanted to tell Malek that he appreciated him. He had watched Malek become less sure of himself and his future, and he wanted him to know that he should be satisfied with the kind of person he was.

Malek shrugged. And then he laughed. "Be careful," he said, "or you'll also pick up my bad habits. My mother says I brag too much." He pushed his hands into his pants pockets, stood still for a time, and watched the moving traffic. "Hadi, you're getting to be like the guy who wrote that book: a philosopher. I think I'm the one who can learn from you now."

"Not really," Hadi said. "It just seems like that's why people need friends: to give some of themselves to each other."

"But that's what you did when you told me we might be able to figure out a way to go to school," Malek said. "I don't know if we can do it, but it's given me something to hope for again."

Hadi knew he had to get back to his side of the street, but he hesitated. His few minutes with Malek were the best of his day, every day. He gave Malek his list of words and told him they could study them together later. And then he said, "So let's keep thinking that we can start school—maybe in the fall."

"Okay. But I still don't think my father will let me do it. Our savings are almost gone. He's at least started trying harder to find work, but everyone turns him down. My brothers and I are doing better, but we still don't bring in as much as we need. I don't see how I can ask to leave my corner, even if it's just a couple of hours earlier."

"So what are you going to do? Move to a different apartment somewhere?"

"Yes. I think so." But then he lifted his head. "My father brought some of his engineering books with him. I've been reading them at night. I probably only understand them about as well as you do your book, but at least I feel like I'm doing something."

The cars had stopped now, but still Malek didn't step off

the curb. It was such a nice morning, with only a few bumpy clouds in a bright sky, and somewhere, not too far away, a rooster was crowing. The bird didn't seem to understand about crowing when the sun came up. Hadi, for a long time, had heard it setting up a racket in spurts all day. But he had always liked hearing it. He could shut his eyes and think he was in the country somewhere, maybe on a farm. He knew very little about farms, but he liked to imagine a peaceful place where there were no car horns and nothing to sell, nothing to worry about.

"Maybe your father can sell things on the street, like my father," Hadi said. "That would mean four of you bringing in money, not just three."

"He won't do it, Hadi. He says it would be a shame to him to do what we do. My mother is disgusted with him. They started yelling at each other last night." Malek looked at the cars, but he had waited too long; the traffic would soon start to move again.

"My mother is feeling better," Hadi said. "But I doubt she'll ever be like she was when we were home and she had her family nearby. But she keeps going, doing what she has to do, and she's trying harder now to make things as good as she can."

But Hadi had come across the street to lift Malek, help him feel a little better. He didn't want to leave with the mood so somber again. "Malek, I've been earning some extra money lately. I could share some of it with you, and you could start taking more home. Your father might feel better if that happened."

"What do you mean, 'extra' money?"

"I do things for the cabbies sometimes. I get cigarettes or food for them. Or I deliver things for them. It's because I'm on that side of the street."

Malek took a long look at Hadi, but the cars had stopped again, so he walked back onto the street. Hadi knew he should cross over now, but instead he waited for Malek's answer about the money.

When Malek came back, Hadi said, "When I have a good day, I keep some of the money, so I can maybe make up for a bad day later. That way my mother isn't disappointed with what I bring home. Come with me for a minute." He walked behind the wall, and Malek followed. Hadi leaned against the wall and took off one of his shoes. He pulled out the bills that he had stuck there, and he held out ten thousand lira. "Here," he said. "Take this much for today."

Malek looked shocked. He stared at Hadi and didn't take the money. "It's what I've worried about," he finally said.

"What?"

"Drugs."

"What are you talking about?"

"I see guys stop sometimes, and you give them little boxes. Rashid has you selling drugs."

"No. I don't sell drugs. Rashid asks me to hand over those boxes to friends of his who stop by. That's all."

"Don't be stupid, Hadi. It's drugs. You know it is."

Hadi looked past Malek. He could see Samir in the street, waving his arms, directing people who had driven into the intersection after the light had changed. The honking had suddenly gone crazy. Sometimes Hadi wished he could run—just set out running and get as far away from this corner as possible. He hadn't known that it could ever be such a trap to him. "You're right," he said. "It's drugs. But I don't sell them. I never see them. Rashid just has me pass the boxes to people."

"You can't do that, Hadi. Do you know what drugs do to people? My brother had a friend who—"

"I know, Malek. I know drugs are bad for people. But what else am I supposed to do? I don't get people started on drugs. I just hand them over—and those people are going to buy them anyway, no matter who delivers them. This world with its bombs and hatred and unfairness decided to make every day of our lives miserable. All I'm doing is fighting back."

"You can't be serious."

"I am serious. And I'll tell you what else. Rashid might know someone who needs a boy to make deliveries. You should find out if you can do the same thing. If we're ever going to get back into school, we need money—and this is a way we can get what we need."

"That makes me sick, Hadi. I'm lowering myself to stand on this corner every day and beg people to buy my tissues, but I won't ever sell drugs. You call it 'delivering,' not selling, but you help the sale happen. You're part of the drug deal. That's wrong and you know it."

"Fine. You're better than I am. But don't ever ask me for money again."

"I didn't ask you for money."

Hadi hardly knew what he was saying. But he didn't want to be accused. And strangely, he was about to cry, which above all, he didn't want to do. Without saying good-bye, he strode into the traffic, set off a blast of horns, and hurried to his side of the street.

When he reached the cabstand, he saw the cabbies looking at him, so he walked to his curb and began going from car to car. And he mumbled to himself, "I saved my mother with that money. And I'm feeding my family. Malek can act like he's better than me, but he'll be out in the street one of these days."

Tears had begun to run down Hadi's face. He wiped them away and kept going, stopping at each car, holding out the boxes. And then suddenly, when a man told him to leave him alone, Hadi threw all four boxes in the man's face and walked away.

He was sick of all this, tired beyond belief, ashamed that he was now a drug dealer, and more than anything, alone. He no longer had a friend.

11

Rashid was angry when Hadi left the cars and walked back to the corner by the cabstand. "You were across the street again," he yelled at Hadi. "What were you doing over there?"

Hadi was in no mood to talk to Rashid, and he didn't want him to see that he had been shedding tears. He looked down, didn't say anything.

"I told you not to go over there. That boy is not your friend. He took your corner." He waited, but Hadi still didn't respond. Rashid lowered his voice, but it remained full of anger. "I have a package for you to deliver today. But I'm paying you nothing for doing it. If my friend gives you something, you can keep that, but I'm tired of you wandering off."

Hadi really didn't care. He was in a trap he couldn't pull himself out of, and now he had lost his hope of teaming with Malek to make things better. It seemed nothing but foolishness that he had convinced himself anything would change.

The next couple of days were agonizing for Hadi. He

watched Malek, but Malek was careful not to look back at him. Hadi thought of walking over and saying he was sorry, but then what? Could he promise that he would stop delivering the boxes? He could only do that if he tried to escape to some other part of town, away from Rashid. But that meant all the problems his family had faced would return, and he couldn't let that happen. But now, with Rashid paying him less, he would soon run out of the money he had been hiding away. The results might end up the same.

For the third evening in a row, Hadi walked to the Dora intersection alone. Malek seemed to wait on purpose, and remained on his corner when Hadi left. Hadi gave his father eighteen thousand pounds, just to start preparing him for worse days ahead. And that night he had trouble falling asleep—something he rarely did. A few hours later he was awake and shaking, the noise and chaos of battle filling his head. He told himself he was all right, but then he thought of all that was going on and lay on the floor feeling utterly miserable, hopeless.

But in the morning he said nothing to Baba about his troubles, and he walked back to his intersection, stood and waited for the cars to stop—and above all, tried not to think. It was an hour or so later when he saw Samir leave the middle of the intersection and walk toward him.

"There's something I need to tell you," Samir said. But then he looked back at the traffic and said, rather loudly, "It doesn't matter whether I'm out there or not—the madness is always the same." He slapped Hadi on the back and laughed, or tried to, and Hadi realized he was trying to make the cabbies think he was only killing time. But Hadi had heard the seriousness in his first words and he knew Samir had something important to say.

Samir lowered his voice. "The police know that Rashid is a drug dealer," he said. "Are you aware of that, Hadi?"

Hadi shrugged. He wanted to ask Samir for help, but he knew better than to admit to anything.

"Hadi, I've seen you hand something to men who stop at this corner, and I know it isn't gum. I've seen you do this several times." He waited, but Hadi still didn't respond. "I think Rashid has you handing off his drugs. Do you have any idea how much trouble you can get into for that?"

"Yes." Hadi looked away, watched the traffic. He heard the usual sound of tires on the pavement, but it all felt new; his place, his corner, was gone, and it seemed as though the cars were about to start piling up on top of him. He didn't know how he had gotten himself into such a complicated mess.

"The police department is watching. One of these days they're going to come sweeping in here, and if they find drugs, it won't be just the taxi drivers who are in trouble. They'll take you in with the others."

"I don't sell drugs."

"I know you don't. But I think you're delivering, and when you do, Rashid drives away. That's to cover himself.

If you get caught, he can say he wasn't involved, and the police will want to know where you're getting the packages. If you tell them that Rashid is your source, your life will be in danger."

Hadi felt his throat tighten.

"I'm sure that Rashid gets his drugs from the drug clans in the Bekaa Valley. Those drug people have power, Hadi. More power than you can imagine. Kamal's people are nothing compared to them. If we pick up Rashid, they'll get him out of jail. And then he'll be looking for you—because you could be a witness against him. Rashid won't be satisfied just to kill you. He'll cut you up, make you suffer. And if he can't find you, he'll look for your father. You won't be safe, Hadi, and neither will your family."

Samir glanced over at the cabbies, and he pretended to laugh again.

"What can I do?"

"I honestly think you would be better off to move away from Beirut, maybe go up north to Jbeil or Tripoli. You need to escape from Rashid and never see the man again. And do it before it's too late."

Samir patted Hadi on the back, laughed again, turned and greeted the other taxi drivers. But then he walked away. Hadi had lost his breath. He had worried about being in trouble, but he hadn't realized, not fully, how far this could go. What could he tell his father, his mother? Would his family really have to move away and try to get started somewhere else? It was too terrible to imagine, and it was probably impossible.

His impulse was to run, to head for the Dora intersection and tell his father everything that Samir had said. But he knew better. He had to finish his day, pretend that nothing had happened.

Hadi kept working, continued to walk to the cars, one at a time, and strangely, everything seemed about the same as always. Most drivers paid him no attention, didn't seem to notice that he was breathless, shaking. A few bought his gum and most didn't, as always. And Rashid, when he came back, seemed to have decided that he had been too hard on Hadi. Maybe he saw how nervous Hadi was, or maybe the other cabbies had told him about Samir coming over to talk with him. For whatever reason, he gave Hadi five thousand pounds and joked with him about being a good delivery boy.

Late in the day, the Risers came by. When Hadi stepped up to their car, Mrs. Riser greeted him with her usual smile, but immediately she asked, "Hadi, are you all right?"

"Yes. I'm just . . . well, I'm fine." She offered him a thousand-pound bill, but Hadi said, "You don't have to give me money. We're friends."

"But we want to—"

"It's all right. I might not be back here tomorrow."

She didn't seem to understand, but Mr. Riser did, and he asked, "Where are you going?"

"I don't know. I might work somewhere else."

But now cars were honking. "We want to help you," Mrs. Riser said. But Mr. Riser was glancing back at the impatient drivers behind him. He said he was sorry, and he drove away.

And now Hadi had lost two more friends.

Hadi couldn't think what he would do now. He could only think that he would finish out the day, and then, if he was going to break with Rashid, he would do so before morning. But when it was almost time to leave, he saw Malek crossing the street. Hadi was relieved to see him come his way. He thought maybe they could talk things out now. But Malek said, "Come with me. Kamal wants to talk to me—and to you."

"How do you know?"

"He sent one of his men to me. Kamal's down this way."

Hadi glanced at Rashid, who was watching, his eyes saying that he wasn't pleased with Malek being there. "I can't leave," Hadi said. "Rashid won't like it."

"I can't say no to Kamal. You can't either."

"Just walk back across the street, and then, in a few minutes, I'll tell Rashid I'm finished for the day, and I'll come to you. Then we can—"

"Kamal wants us now."

Hadi was caught. Kamal was dangerous and Rashid was worse. But he didn't want to get Malek into trouble. So Hadi walked to Rashid and said, "Can I put my gum in the cabinet? It's time for me to go meet my father."

"Aren't you quitting early?"

"Not really. The sun stays up a little longer now, but it's about the time I usually stop."

"Who decides that? You, or that Malek kid from across the street?"

Hadi knew this was all about control. It was Rashid who wanted to tell him when to be there, when to quit. But Hadi wasn't coming back. "I'll see you in the morning," he said, and he walked away with Malek. He hoped Rashid wasn't coming after him. But he had to go.

The boys walked south along the busy street. There was a sidewalk, but cars were parked on it, so they had to wind their way in and out of traffic. Near the next corner, at the mouth of an alley, a man was standing, waiting. Hadi realized it must be Kamal.

"What took you so long to get here?" Kamal asked, and Hadi heard the fury in his voice. Without waiting for an answer, Kamal said, "Come with me." He turned and walked deeper into the alley. He looked at Hadi. "Malek told you to clear off his corner. Why are you still here?"

"I work the other side of the street now. I don't—"

"That doesn't matter. I told you to leave."

Hadi heard the rage and decided not to say anything else.

"One of my men has seen you still talking to Malek, and today you talked to that policeman from the intersection. Samir. What were you talking about?"

Hadi tried to sound calm when he said, "Just talking. He's friendly."

"I asked you, what were you talking about?"

"I can't remember. How bad the traffic is and things like that."

Kamal stepped closer. "We hear things. Rumors go around. And what we hear lately is that the police are after me." Kamal kept watching Hadi, as though he wanted to see the effect of his words. Hadi tried to look back at him, steady, not show any reaction. "Did Samir ask you about me?"

"No."

"You're lying. I think he wants you to be a witness against me. Malek's been complaining to you about me, hasn't he?"

"No." Hadi glanced at Malek and saw how frightened he was, the blood gone from his face. "Samir didn't say one word about anything like that. That's the truth."

Hadi kept looking Kamal straight in the eye, and he thought the man believed him this time.

"Maybe he did and maybe he didn't," Kamal said. "But from now on you work for me. You won't be crossing the street to waste Malek's time. I'll give you a place to work, and you better work hard." He slammed his fist into his palm, as if to demonstrate his power. He was not a big man, but Hadi felt his force. He filled up his leather coat with big shoulders, and yet it was his voice, full of venom, that was most frightening.

Hadi hesitated, but then said, "I won't work at this intersection anymore. I'll leave today and find a different place in some other part of the city. Or maybe move to a new city."

"You don't listen very well, do you?" He held his fist out, close to Hadi's face. "I just told you, you work for me now and I'll decide where you go. Where do you get your gum now?"

"My father gets it for me."

"Where?"

"At a shop."

"What does your father do?"

"He sells things on the street, the same as me." But Hadi knew instantly he had said the wrong thing. He had revealed too much.

"Where?"

"I don't know what it's called. It's just another intersection." There was no way he was going to tell Kamal where his father worked.

"You're going with me. Right now. We're going to find your father. He's going to work for me too."

"Rashid, the taxi driver, wants me on the corner where the cabstand is," he said. "He won't like you taking me away. You better be careful about that." This stopped Kamal for the moment, so Hadi went on. "He's a tough guy. He'll come after you and he'll—"

Kamal grabbed the front of Hadi's jacket. He shoved Hadi against the building behind him. Hadi hit the back of his head, hard, and everything swirled for a moment as he sank to the pavement. He was just starting to get his vision back when Kamal grabbed him by his jacket and pulled him up. "Don't threaten me, you little swine. I'll kill you right here."

Hadi tried to stand on his feet, but Kamal was lifting him onto his toes. Then suddenly he struck him across the face with the back of his hand and Hadi's knees gave way. Kamal let him fall onto the grimy street. Hadi curled up, tried to get his breath, but Kamal kicked him hard in the back, the pain shooting all through his body.

By then Malek was yelling, "No! Don't kill him! Don't kill him!"

But Kamal kicked Hadi again, harder.

Suddenly Malek drove his shoulder into Kamal, surprised him and knocked him back. "Run, Hadi," Malek gasped.

Hadi jumped up, still dizzy. He doubted that running would get him anywhere, but he ran anyway. Kamal had already cast Malek aside, and he was running after Hadi, but the delay had been enough that Hadi made it out of the alley ahead of Kamal, and without looking, he charged into the middle of the traffic. He heard brakes screech, but he kept going. By the time he was across the street, he couldn't hear Kamal behind him. Maybe the man had not wanted to run into the traffic, or maybe he didn't want to be seen chasing a kid. All Hadi knew was that he had to keep running.

There was another alley on the opposite side of the street, and Hadi ran down it. Then, when he saw an open door, he dodged into a building. It was an apartment house—a dark, stinking place—but Hadi kept going and found his way out the front door onto another street. Then he turned left and ran through that street, kept finding alleys and streets angling this way and that. The alleys were full of dumpsters, garbage cans, and plastic sacks piled high. A man sitting on a back step smoking a cigarette watched Hadi run by and yelled something at him. Hadi paid no attention. He was looking back from time to time, and he still saw no sign of Kamal. Maybe Kamal had turned back and was taking out his anger on Malek. Maybe he would force Malek to tell him where Baba worked. Malek knew about the Dora intersection. Hadi had to get there first.

When he broke onto a busier street, Hadi realized something else: people were watching him. He felt the back of his head and then looked at his hand. It was covered with blood. The sight of the blood took some of his strength away. He had run all out at first, but now his legs, his lungs couldn't keep up the pace. There was also a cloudiness in his vision, and he was feeling the pain in his back.

So Hadi slowed to a walk, still keeping to back streets, never heading directly west, but always toward Dora. After he covered a few more blocks, he realized he had to get to Garo at the fruit stand. If he got that far, he would be close to the Dora intersection, but he needed help, and the only person he could think of to help him was Garo.

So Hadi crossed Mirna Chalhoui Highway and continued on into Bourj Hammoud. By now he was wobbling with each step, and he was not seeing anything very clearly. But if Garo could stop his bleeding, Hadi could make it to his father. He had to.

Hadi's feet seemed to know the way better than he did and kept him going, but all along the busy street, people turned to look at him. A woman came up behind him and said, "Young man, you're hurt. You need—"

"I know. I'll be all right. I have a friend down this way."

"But you're bleeding—bad."

"I know." And now he could see that the blood had worked its way under his jacket and around to the front of his shirt.

Two more people asked him whether he needed help. Each time he said that he was all right and he kept going. When he finally reached the fruit stand, he was almost finished. He stopped a few feet away from Garo, and when he did, his knees gave way. He sank to the sidewalk. "I'm hurt," he said.

Garo had been sitting with his eyes closed, probably asleep. But his eyes opened wide now. "Hadi," he said, "what's happened to you?"

Hadi didn't try to explain. He only pointed to his head.

Garo, slow in his heaviness, stood up. He grabbed Hadi, pulled him up and hugged him to his chest. He lifted him and carried him through the little fruit stand and the curtain that hung at the back. There were boxes back there and a cabinet, and the smell of rotting fruit so thick that it nauseated Hadi. It had been coming for a while, but finally Hadi couldn't hold back. He vomited, his empty stomach gushing mostly liquid.

Garo held him.

"I'm sorry," Hadi said. "I'm sorry."

"It's all right."

But Hadi was losing his battle with consciousness. He felt himself slipping down, even as Garo tried to grasp him.

12

"Can you hear what I'm saying?" Garo was asking, his face close, his labored breath brushing Hadi's cheek.

Hadi opened his eyes. It took him a second or two to remember where he was. He was sitting in a wooden chair behind Garo's fruit stand. "Yes," he finally managed to say.

"Thanks be to God," Garo muttered. "We must clean you up and get a bandage on you to stop the bleeding."

And then Hadi remembered. "I have to hurry," he said. "I have to find my father."

"Why must you hurry?"

"Someone might hurt him."

"The same one who hurt you?"

"Yes."

"What's happening, Hadi? Who did this to you?"

"I can't talk about it."

"All right. But we have to take care of this before you do anything else." Garo moved around Hadi in his composed way, as though life for him, regardless of what was happening, was a matter of deliberate motion, always steady. "Rest for a minute. I must go into my house and get some things to bandage you, or you won't make it to your father."

Hadi thought he couldn't wait. He feared that Kamal had forced Malek to tell him where Baba worked and was already on his way to the Dora intersection.

But he did wait—partly because he wasn't sure his legs would carry him and partly because his friend Garo was taking care of him. He also knew that it was better not to walk down the street all covered in blood.

Garo appeared after a few minutes. Hadi hadn't known that Garo lived in the building behind his fruit stand. But he came from there, carrying a small pail of water and some white rags. "Let's take your jacket and shirt off," he said.

"It's okay. Just wash the blood away."

"Your clothes are full of blood too. I'll get you something else to wear." He was unzipping Hadi's jacket, so Hadi helped him, and they took off his jacket, then pulled his shirt over his head. Hadi finally saw how soaked with blood his clothes were, and that scared him. He didn't know how much blood he could lose and still live. He didn't know whether he was still bleeding.

"Nothing bleeds so bad as the head," Garo was telling him. "But now that I see the wound, it's not so bad as you might think. You'll be all right."

And then he wet one of the rags and began to wipe

Hadi's hair and neck. When he rinsed the rag in the pail of water, it turned pink immediately. Hadi found himself settling back in the chair. The warmth of the water and the gentleness of the old man's touch were soothing to Hadi.

"My family lived in Aleppo before they came here," Garo said as he worked.

This took Hadi by surprise. Garo knew that Hadi had lived in Aleppo, but Garo had never mentioned that his own family had lived there.

"Do you know about the Armenians, Hadi?" Garo asked.

"I know they live in Bourj Hammoud."

"Yes. And I am Armenian. At one time, in this part of the city, we were all Armenian, but that's changed." Hadi couldn't imagine why Garo thought it was important to talk about that now. "I want to tell you a little about our history," Garo continued. "There are some things you need to know."

Hadi took a long breath. "All right," he said.

"In 1915, the Turks tried to destroy Armenians. We call that the 'genocide.' Do you know what that means?"

"No."

"'Genocide' is killing all the people of a certain group or nation. The Turks wanted to rid themselves of all of us. So we fled. We went everywhere. When I say that, you understand, I wasn't born yet. But my grandfather took my father and his other children to Syria, to Aleppo. They stayed . . . I don't know exactly . . . maybe ten years or so. And then they decided they might have better opportunities here in Beirut.

So they came here, and I was born in Bourj Hammoud. But it's not my home—not really."

Hadi didn't understand that, but he didn't say so.

"So you see what I'm telling you? We're refugees, the same as you, and I might well have been a Syrian citizen if my family had stayed in Aleppo. But when Syrians come here now, some of my people forget this and resent new refugees living among us—ones with a different religion and different heritage. It's the same everywhere. People are forced to leave a place because of war, or because they are attacked, or because of famine and bad crops. And then, when they find a new place, some people say, 'We don't want you.' And sometimes they break open the heads of the new people. I wish it were not so."

Hadi thought he understood what Garo was saying to him. Maybe it was why Garo gave him food at such a low price, and maybe it was why he was folding a clean rag into a narrow strip and tying the strip tight around Hadi's head.

"It's not bleeding much now, Hadi. But leave this rag on for a few hours—or maybe until tomorrow. Are you feeling stronger now?"

"Yes."

"Still, sit for a minute or two and I'll get you something to wear. Eat this banana while I'm gone. You need some food to rebuild your strength."

So Hadi stayed, and he ate the banana—a fresh one that tasted better than the brown ones he usually got from

Garo. He knew he had to get going, but he was thinking more clearly now. He needed to regain some strength, and he knew that he couldn't put his bloody clothes back on. He hoped Kamal, if he had driven to the Dora intersection, wouldn't know how to identify Baba. In fact, the real danger might come when Hadi approached his father on the street.

Hadi had time now, and enough concentration, to think about Malek throwing his shoulder into Kamal, knocking him back. It made Hadi feel sick again to think what Kamal might have done to him by now. He considered going back to see what he could do, but he knew that was impossible.

When Garo returned, he had a shirt and jacket. Hadi thought they looked new. He must have bought them in one of the shops along the street. The shirt was light blue, the jacket a darker blue. Hadi liked them both. He hadn't worn new clothes in many years.

As Garo helped Hadi get the shirt over his head without pulling the bandage loose, he said, "Hadi, my family came to Beirut with nothing, but my father set up a little stand like this one on a street corner, and he sold things sort of the way you and your father do. In time he was able to set up a shop of his own. He sold a few things he thought people wanted for their homes, and eventually he had a whole hardware store: tools, pipes, light fixtures, sinks—everything. I worked for him, and then he turned the business over to me. I ran that store for many years, but a few years ago my wife passed away, and my children were all married, so I sold

　　　　　　　　　　　　　　　　　　　　DEAN HUGHES

the business. But I didn't like sitting home alone. I went back to our beginning, and I opened this little fruit stand. It's a chance to talk to people all day long. And it's a chance to remember who I am."

"I need to go, Garo. I want to talk to you more about all those things, but right now I need to go."

"I understand. But listen to what I've been telling you. We came with nothing, and we did what we had to do to make a living. After a time we had a shop, and then a big store. We've had good lives here. I know things are different now, maybe worse, but I'm telling you that you can find a way forward—even when people beat you over the head."

"All right." But Hadi could only think that he had tried for a long time and things had merely gotten worse. Garo had no idea how much trouble he was in.

"Come to me when you need my help. It's what we should do: help each other."

"Thank you, Garo. *Allah yehmik.*"

"And may Jesus bless you, Hadi." He patted Hadi on the shoulder, smiled at him, his whole face folding into wrinkles.

Hadi wished he could tell Garo everything, then ask for his advice. But he had to go. When he stood, he felt more strength in his legs. So he said goodbye and hurried down the street. He was self-conscious about the rag tied around his head, but he didn't look at people. He just kept walking as fast as he could, and he soon realized his legs were not as strong as he had thought. And now he was feeling more pain in his back.

His nervousness heightened as he neared the Dora intersection. Dora was a huge roundabout with several streets joining and a freeway passing over the top. Cars and trucks and motorbikes were all crushed together, and movement was slow. The place was not just busy; the mood of the drivers was frantic. It was the kind of chaos that would hide a scuffle if Kamal or his men were waiting to grab him and Baba.

Hadi spotted his father on his usual corner. He seemed to be all right. But Hadi didn't rush to him. He watched for Kamal or the man in the black jacket. They could be hiding, watching for Hadi. Or maybe they had come and gone. Maybe Hadi's delay in getting there had been just the right thing.

After five minutes or so, Hadi still couldn't see Kamal, so he began to walk toward Baba, watching closely, and when he reached him, he took a last look around. By then Baba was saying, "Hadi, what happened to you?"

There was so much to tell, and most of it Hadi didn't want to admit. But right now they needed to get away from this intersection.

"We have to leave," he said. "Kamal beat up on me. He might still be looking for me—and for you. And there are other things going on. There's a lot I have to tell you."

Hadi saw the grim look on his father's face. His head

was dropping down, his eyes narrowing. "Hadi, I haven't sold much today. I need to stay a while and—"

"No. We can't let him find us." Hadi didn't know how to explain, quickly, that Rashid might also be after them before long. So he said only, "There are people who might want to *kill* us—not just you and me but our whole family. We have to go."

"Hadi, I don't understand. What's—"

"I'll tell you everything when we're on the bus. But we need to get off this corner."

Baba finally seemed to feel Hadi's fear. "All right. We'll go." But he took a step and then stopped. "I have to turn these things in." He had been selling toy cars and trucks. "We'll have to hurry to the shop."

"Baba, just throw them away. I don't think you can come back here again."

For a couple of seconds Baba stared at Hadi. He had no way of knowing how completely their lives were about to change.

"I can't throw them away," he said, and Hadi understood. To Baba, there were things that were wrong, and he wouldn't do them. He and Hadi hurried to the little shop where Baba picked up his items for sale each morning. He left the toys on a shelf he used each night, and then he and Hadi walked to the bus stop. Hadi wanted to run, but he also didn't want to call attention to himself and his father.

They crossed two streets and worked their way through

the cars that were bogged down in the traffic. When they reached the bus stop, Hadi kept twisting to look up and down the street. But no one had followed them—no one he could see.

On the bus, Baba finally looked at Hadi, obviously expecting an explanation.

"Baba, Kamal told me that I had to work for him, and I told him no. He threw me into a wall and cut my head, but I ran away, and he chased after me. I don't know if he'll try to find me, but I think he will, and I know he won't let me work in his part of town."

"He doesn't know me. Maybe I can still—"

"But that's only part of the problem." Hadi lowered his head, didn't look at Baba when he said, "I . . . I gave drugs to people. I didn't sell them. I only passed them along. A man asked me to do it, and then—"

"I knew it was drugs," Baba whispered. "I knew you were doing too well, always bringing home more money than you had before. But it helped us so much, I didn't want to ask you too many questions. I'm as much at fault as you are."

Hadi could hardly believe his father would forgive him, even accept some of the guilt. He felt enormously relieved. "Mama needed medicine and—"

"I know. But what's going to happen to us now?"

"I can't go back to my intersection—because of Kamal— but when I don't show up in the morning, I think the drug dealer—Rashid—will start looking for me. He told me I had to keep working for him. He's afraid I'll be a witness for the police if he gets arrested, so he wants to keep me under his control. He told me if I ever turned against him, his people would find me and kill me. And our family, too. I'm sorry, Baba. I don't know what we can do. I think we have to leave. Go to another city."

Baba looked destroyed. "We're at the end, Hadi. We've tried everything to keep going, and now I can't even sell those worthless toys on the street. I don't know what to do."

"Samir—the policeman at our intersection—told me we should move to Jbeil or Tripoli and start over there."

"How do we get there, Hadi? Walk? We don't have enough money to take a bus that far. Not all of us. And how do we find a place to live?"

Hadi had only thought about getting Baba away from the Dora intersection. He hadn't thought what might come next. "Will the charity help us?"

"They won't relocate us. Everyone in our neighborhood is asking for help, and the charities are running out of money."

Hadi felt the weight of all this, felt himself sink into the plastic seat of the bus. "I did this," he said.

"You were trying to help us, son, trying to help your mother."

But that didn't matter. It didn't change anything.

"Maybe we can try working on the other side of town," Baba said. "Maybe in Hamra. These men might not look for us if they realize we've cleared away from their part of the city."

"And then we'll face gangs like Kamal's in Hamra."

"But it's the only thing I can think of. We can't miss a day on the street or we'll be out of food again in just a few days."

"I have some money. I kept some back and hid it in my shoe."

"How much?"

"I can't remember exactly. More than forty thousand. It's enough to buy food for a while, maybe a week. But not enough to travel to another city and get us started there." He reached for his shoe, to get it out.

"That's all right. Just keep what you have for now. We'll use it as we have to. You'll have to hide at home, and I'll take Khaled, and we'll work in Hamra."

"Baba, if you're going to Hamra, I'm going with you. We'll have to take a chance—and hope Rashid won't find me."

"Maybe. I don't know. Let me think."

They lapsed into silence. Hadi was glad not to think anymore. His head was throbbing, and the pain in his back made it hard for him to lean against the seat. He had decided not to tell Baba about any of that, but he had something else on his mind. He was still worried about Malek. He thought of the stories he had heard about boys being found in alleys, beaten to death. He thought of Malek's body, like little Marwa's, broken and bent.

13

When Hadi stepped into the room, at home, Mama saw the band around his head and looked startled. "Oh, Hadi, what's happened to you?" She hurried to him, then grasped his shoulders and looked into his face.

"It's nothing. I just bumped the back of my head."

She moved around behind him and said, "Blood has soaked through the cloth. This was more than a 'bump,' Hadi."

Hadi loved that she was touching him, that her voice sounded so concerned. She was much more alive than she had been when her pain had been so bad. He hated to think that that could all change again. "It's nothing," Hadi said. "I stumbled and hit my head against a wall. I should have been more careful. But it's not serious. I can still go back to work tomorrow."

She stepped back in front of him, took hold of his shoulders again, and stared into his face. "Did someone hurt you, Hadi?"

"No. I just tripped. But Garo—the one who sells me fruits and vegetables—put this bandage around my head. I can probably take it off now."

"No. Leave it. Don't take a chance yet."

Baba had stayed out of all this, but now he said, "We're thinking we'll stay closer to home tomorrow—in case Hadi gets tired. We want to try Hamra anyway—and see whether we can't make a little more money over there among all those rich people."

"You've done well lately. We've had more food. Maybe you shouldn't leave the corners where you've worked so long."

"I know. We might go back. But for now we'll try Hamra."

Mama glanced at Hadi and then back at Baba. Hadi could see that she was sensing something was wrong. She surely remembered why they had decided to cross the city to Dora and Bauchrieh in the first place.

Hadi heard Baba try to keep his voice light as he said, "We did all right today." Hadi, on the bus, had turned over his money from that day, and with the 5,000 from Rashid and a tip from the drug customer, he had made 15,500. Baba had added another 7,000. "I'll get some extra groceries tonight. And then we'll just see how we do in Hamra tomorrow."

Hadi could bring some of his money out each day, to go with what he received on the street. And fortunately, Mama didn't ask what they were going to sell. It was too expensive and dangerous to cross the city just to bring back gum and other items to sell in Hamra. They would have to beg money from people until they could find a new source for things to sell.

Aram came to Hadi and wrapped his arms around his leg. "I'm sorry you hurt your head," Aram whispered.

Hadi touched Aram's hair, then knelt down by him. "Thank you, Aram. I love you. But don't worry; it's not too bad."

The girls were sitting on the floor together. They had been playing, but now they were all looking up at Hadi. "You've got blood on your head," Aliya said. "It makes me want to puke." Rabia and Samira laughed. But when Mama looked her way, Aliya ducked her head. "I'm only joking," she said.

Mama looked at Hadi again. "Tell me this. Where did you get those new clothes?"

"Garo bought them for me. I got blood on my shirt and jacket."

"Why did he do that? Do we have to pay him?"

"No. He wanted to help me. We're friends."

Mama looked doubtful. "We should pay him," she said.

"He's Armenian," Hadi told her. "His people had to leave their country. They lived in Aleppo before they came here. He understands about being a refugee. He's a kind man."

Baba said, "Mama, there are kind people in this world. We can't forget that."

"I do forget it," Mama said. "I hope you'll tell him how grateful we are."

Hadi was relieved that Mama hadn't asked too many questions and that so far he hadn't had to scare her with Rashid's threats. He glanced at Baba, who gave Hadi a little nod and then said, "Since we're staying so close, we thought we would take Khaled with us tomorrow. He can start helping us now."

Khaled had been sitting in a corner, paying little attention, but now he jumped up. "Yes. I want to go with you."

"All right," Baba said. He and Hadi had talked on the way home about taking Khaled with them. Grown men who tried to beg in the streets didn't do well unless they were amputees or were sitting in wheelchairs. Children sometimes did better, and Khaled looked even younger than he was.

Khaled was excited. "I'll earn lots of money," he said. "I'll work hard."

Hadi needed to talk to him, but not in front of everyone, so he volunteered to go grocery shopping. When Mama protested, he said he would take Khaled, who could carry everything up their three flights of stairs. So Hadi pulled the rag off his head and showed his mother that his wound wasn't bleeding now, and Baba said it was all right.

Hadi and Khaled walked down the dark stairs. When they reached the street, Hadi said, "It won't be easy in Hamra. It won't be the same as we've done before. You won't have anything to sell. You'll have to ask people for money."

"Can't I sell gum?"

"We don't have any over here. Maybe we can find a place to get it cheap, but for tomorrow we'll just have to try begging."

"I wanted to sell gum."

"I know. But we can't help it."

"What will I say to people?"

So Hadi explained the way he should approach the cars, stop at the drivers' windows, and hold both hands out, cupped. "But don't smile. Look sad. If they don't give you anything, you can do this." He raised his hand to his mouth, as if eating. It was what Hadi had seen other children do sometimes as he had walked to Dora from his intersection. "If the window is open, say, 'I'm hungry,' or 'My family is hungry. Please help us.' If they don't tell you to leave them alone, you can keep saying things. Like, 'Have you a coin or two that you can spare? That's all I ask.'"

"I thought you got a thousand pounds most of the time."

"That's for gum. But when you have nothing to sell, you have to take what you can get."

"You said that people are mean sometimes."

"Yes. Expect it. They'll say, 'Why don't you Syrians go back where you belong?' Things like that. But don't listen to them. Just go to the next car."

"Why do we have to do this? Why can't Baba find a job?" Khaled sounded less excited now.

"We don't have legal papers, Khaled. Refugees are only

allowed to do hard labor, but most of those jobs go to younger men. Baba doesn't look so young anymore."

Hadi could see in Khaled's eyes that he was understanding all this for the first time—or trying to. He had wanted to get out of the house, had wanted to work like his big brother, but now he seemed to be grasping what he would actually have to do.

The narrow street was dark now, and not many people were outside. Hadi and Khaled walked by a little shop where a Pakistani man sold chips and sodas and chocolate bars. There were no customers—never were, it seemed—and Hadi always wondered how the man stayed in business. Hadi bought groceries in a larger store farther down the street.

"Don't be scared," Hadi told Khaled on the way back. "Just keep trying and a few people will give you money. And you'll be proud of yourself when you go home at night. Be careful, though. If men or older boys approach you and tell you that you can't work on a certain corner, just walk away. Don't argue. And if any men want you to go with them, don't do it, no matter what they say."

"Can we stay together tomorrow, so I can learn what to do?"

"I'll show you in the beginning, and we'll always stay close to each other."

"Okay." And that seemed to relax Khaled a little. But Hadi couldn't relax. All evening he worried about what the next day would bring.

• • • •

In the morning Baba and the two boys took a bus from Cola to the Corniche—a beautiful street and walkway along the sea. There were tall buildings there, beautiful hotels and office buildings. It was only two or three miles from Cola, but it was a street Khaled had never seen. "Look at that place. It's made of glass," he said. And he watched the people: men at the beach in swimming suits or women with their heads covered, sitting next to their husbands. Some men fished with long fishing poles and some played a game, hitting a ball over a net with their hands. Khaled was amazed by everything, commented on it all, and Hadi realized how long the boy had been cooped up in Cola in that dark, stinking apartment.

"Look at all those flowers," Khaled said.

Baba told him, "It's what Mama calls majnouneh. We had one behind our building in Aleppo. Hadi and I called it our flower tree."

It was what Hadi loved most here: flower trees in red and pink and purple, all sorts of other flowers, and palm trees. It seemed like heaven. It was a beautiful day, too, with big clouds floating by and no rain. At least Khaled didn't have to make his start on a day when rain was pouring down. It was probably also good that he had no idea of the dangers that might be waiting for them.

When the three got off the bus, they walked up the hill

from the Corniche to Hamra Street, a long stretch that ran through the entire area. It was a fancy part of town, with lots of nice shops, clubs, bars, restaurants.

"People don't throw garbage in the streets here," Khaled said.

"Or if they do, someone comes around and cleans it up," Baba told him. "Rich people shop here, and they don't want to step over trash."

They walked past the American University of Beirut, and Hadi said, "There's lot of traffic along here, but someone is working every corner." There were vendors everywhere, most of them children selling roses not only at the car windows but to pedestrians. There were also grown men selling the sorts of items that Baba had been selling at the Dora intersection.

"No one's begging," Hadi told his father.

"I know. That's what I've been noticing. That probably means the vendors are supplied by the street gangs. I'm sure the good corners are assigned by the same people."

"What can we do?"

"I'm thinking that we should get off Hamra Street but stay close to the university. The students are rich kids, mostly. And maybe they don't hate Syrians so much as the people who shop here probably do."

Baba turned at the next corner, and they found a quieter area with narrower streets. Baba kept looking and finally said, "You boys work this corner and I'll go up another street or two. I might look to see whether I can buy something cheap that I can resell."

"Look to see whether you can find Chiclets," Hadi said.

"I will. But you boys stay right here. Don't leave this corner unless someone comes along and threatens you. If you have to leave, come to me. Otherwise, I'll check back with you in a while."

"All right," Hadi said. But he wondered about Rashid. He might not realize that Hadi wasn't coming back—at least for a day or two. Or would Kamal say something to him? If either one of them put the word out to watch for him, would anyone in this area be able to figure out who he was? Or would they send the people who had watched him in Bauchrieh? Baba had been fairly sure they would be safe in Hamra, but he hadn't heard Rashid's threats. Still, Baba was right; they had to eat.

So Hadi walked to the corner and stood at the curb. Khaled followed him. "Stay with me this first time we go to the cars," he told his brother. "Just watch what I do. And listen. Don't say anything."

Hadi stood at the corner and waited. He was surprised when the cars stopped without running the red light. Maybe the police enforced the law on this side of the city. "All right, let's go," Hadi told Khaled. *"Yallah."*

When they approached the cars, he did as he had told Khaled the night before; he held his palms out, kept his head down, and when he got no response, he motioned to his mouth to show that he was hungry. He tried to look sad, but he didn't overact, and as he had done with the gum, when they ignored him, he moved on.

But Hadi hated doing this. It was demeaning. Baba had always told him to pay for the food Garo gave him, not to beg—and now he was playacting, claiming he was hungry when he wasn't. But he told himself he would be hungry, his whole family would be, if he didn't take home what money he could.

The cars were mostly bigger, nicer than on the other side of town, and the drivers were usually better dressed, but their reaction was the same as in Bauchrieh. When Hadi came to a man who had his window open and his hand out the window holding a cigarette, Hadi said, "Sir, my brother and I are hungry. My family is hungry. Could you spare a coin or two to help us?"

The man smiled, but he didn't look at Hadi. "You people always say you're hungry, but you look like you've had plenty to eat."

Hadi didn't respond. He just walked away. "We do get hungry," Khaled told Hadi as he followed him to the next car.

"I know. But I told you, don't argue with them. It's what they believe, and you can't talk them out of it. Are you ready to go on your own now?"

"Not yet."

So they worked their way through the cars three, then four times, until a young man finally gave Hadi a five-hundred-pound coin and said something in a language Hadi didn't understand. Baba had said that all the students at the university spoke English.

When they walked back to the curb, Khaled said to Hadi, "I thought more people would give us money."

"We have to figure this out," Hadi told him, and he tried to sound calm, but he was worried. They needed to do better. "I think that man was a student. Maybe those are the ones we should talk to. Most of the students are walking in this area, not driving cars. Let's try to stop them on the sidewalk."

Hadi tried to step in front of younger people who came by, so he could get them to stop. Most shook their heads and walked around him, but he picked up a few coins that way. It wasn't much, but it was a bit of an improvement.

Finally, one young woman stopped and listened to Hadi. She looked foreign. She had blond hair, and she spoke Arabic with a strange sound to it, like a little melody. She smiled and said, "Tell me the truth. Are you really hungry?"

Her sincere question embarrassed Hadi. He answered honestly. "Not right now, but our family needs to eat, and this is the only way we can take money home tonight to buy food for our little sisters and brothers."

"I didn't expect you to say that," she said. "Is this your brother?"

"Yes."

She looked at Khaled. "You're a handsome boy," she

said. "You'll have lots of girlfriends someday."

Hadi watched Khaled blush. The girl was pretty.

"Well, boys, I don't have much money, but I want your brothers and sisters to eat tonight. She pulled out a five-thousand-pound bill from her purse. She handed it to Hadi, and then she gave Khaled another five thousand. "Get yourselves a sandwich for lunch, if you can find one for that price around here. You'll have to cut the sandwich in half. I don't have enough money to buy two."

"*Allah yehmiki,*" Hadi said, and he meant it. Khaled repeated the same blessing.

She patted Khaled on the shoulder. "Good luck to both of you." She smiled and walked away.

Hadi was amazed. He turned to Khaled. "You won't see that happen very often. But we won't have lunch. We'll take all of it home. You speak to the next person who comes along. That woman liked the way you look."

"I'll just listen again until—"

"No. You have to start. See that man coming up the street? He looks like a student. Stop him. I'll walk away and let you do it on your own."

"I can't, Hadi. I'm too scared."

"You've been telling me all winter that you want to go with us. This is your chance to get started."

Hadi walked a few paces off.

Khaled stood stiffly and waited. Hadi remembered his own first attempts, how frightened he had been. He felt sorry for Khaled, but the boy had to do this. What Hadi knew was that things might get much worse from now on, and Khaled would have to grow up fast. He hated to push the boy and make him uncomfortable, but what choice did he have?

14

Hadi watched as Khaled waited for the young man approaching him on the sidewalk. But Khaled didn't step in front of the man. He did look at him, but at the last second he turned away, and once the man had passed, he twisted around, looked at Hadi, and shook his head. As Hadi walked to him, Khaled said, "I can't do it."

Hadi felt bad to see how miserable Khaled looked, but he said, "Yes, you can. And you *will* do it. Would you rather go home and sit in the house all day with your sisters and your baby brothers?"

"No."

"Then quit acting like *you're* a baby."

"I'm not a baby!" Khaled said, but his voice cracked, and he began to cry. He turned away and wiped his face with his sleeve.

Hadi felt sorry for him, but he was angry at the same time. He had stuck it out for two years, showing up every day, whether he wanted to or not. "Khaled, you don't understand. You tell me how hungry you are sometimes, but the only reason you get anything to eat is because Baba and I have been doing this for you. I told you that you wouldn't like it. I don't like it either. But it's what we have to do—or none of us eat."

"I couldn't remember what I was supposed to say."

"Just say, 'Could you help me? I'm hungry. My whole family is hungry.' And then he'll say no and keep walking. But that doesn't matter. You keep asking, over and over, and a few people will give you coins and you thank them. That's all we have, Khaled. It's the only thing we can do. It doesn't do any good to wish things were different." But Khaled's tears hadn't stopped, and Hadi was starting to wish he hadn't been so stern with him. "It's hard at first," he added, more gently, "but it gets easier. And after a while, you don't think, you don't feel. And one day is exactly like all the others. The only thing you remember is that your mother and brothers and sisters will have something to eat at night."

"Show me again."

"No, Khaled. You have to do it yourself. It's the only way you can get used to it. Look at that woman coming up the street. She's probably a student. She might be like that other one who was so nice to us. Step in front of her and say, 'Can you help me? I'm hungry.'"

Khaled turned to look and Hadi stepped away. Khaled was still crying, and Hadi doubted he would do anything.

But he did step in front of her, and she did stop. He said something so low and muffled that Hadi couldn't understand him. But the woman, who was wearing a bright-pink hijab, asked, "Are you all right?"

"I'm hungry. My family is hungry," Khaled muttered.

"That's too bad," the young woman said, but she didn't open her purse. "Are you Syrian?"

"Yes."

"Do you have a home?"

"No," Khaled said. "I mean, yes. A room."

"For how many?"

Khaled had probably never counted. He didn't answer.

The woman looked concerned. She had an accent of some kind. Hadi thought she must be from another country. She wore dark-rimmed glasses, which made her look serious, but she was dressed in jeans and tennis shoes. "How many brothers and sisters do you have?" she asked.

"Three brothers. Three sisters."

"So there are seven of you, and do both of your parents live with you?"

"Yes."

"So nine. And you live in one room?"

"Yes." She was still watching Khaled carefully, probably wondering about his tears. In the background cars were honking, as always, and people on the sidewalk were streaming around the two. Hadi had not expected anything like this. Some people had asked him at times if he was okay, but almost no one had ever asked him about his family. It was Khaled's tears, he thought, that had prompted all her questions.

"Is that your brother over there?" the woman asked.

"Yes." Khaled looked around, desperation in his face, as though he had no idea what he was supposed to do now.

Hadi nodded to the woman. And then she waved him over. "Why was your brother crying?" she asked.

"He was scared. He hasn't asked people for money before."

The woman took a long look at Hadi, and he liked the softness of her eyes. She pulled her backpack off her shoulder and opened it. "I want to give you a little money. I'm just wondering whether there isn't something else you can do besides stop people on the street. Aren't there groups that help refugees?"

"Yes. But they're running out of money. They can't help us very much."

"I can understand that," she said. She had found her purse by then. She pulled out three thousand pounds and handed the bills to Khaled, but then she touched his hair, smoothed it a little. "I'm so sorry I can't do more," she said.

She placed her hand over her heart, bowed her head toward Hadi, and she wished him well. Hadi thanked her, blessed her, and then Khaled did too. As she walked away, she smiled and gave them a little wave. The boys stood on the sidewalk for a time and watched her go. Hadi was thankful that she was the first person Khaled had stopped.

"You did well," Hadi told Khaled. "Now do it again. Just don't think that most people will treat you that way." Then he laughed. "Keep crying if you can. I think she liked that."

"I'm not crying!" Khaled said. He wiped his eyes with his shirtsleeve again.

"I'm sorry. I know how scary it is, but I'm thinking it might be easier if I'm not here to listen."

"No. I want you here."

"I know. But you'll learn more if you do it by yourself. So I'm going to leave you on your own. I'm going to cross the street and talk to people over there. But I'll be close all the time."

Khaled stared at Hadi for a few seconds, as though he were about to protest, but then he looked down and said, "All right. I'll try."

So Hadi crossed the street, but he kept an eye on Khaled, who continued to stop people. Most brushed past him, and those who slowed to hear what he had to say usually shook their heads and then walked on by. But Hadi did see him get a few coins.

Hadi also received some coins and a one-thousand-pound bill, but he knew it was not going to amount to much. At least they had the money the two young women had given them.

But Hadi had other worries. He kept watching for Kamal or Rashid, or anyone who might be working for them. He saw a rough-looking guy stop near his corner and take a long look at him, but then he moved on. Hadi knew the man could be working for a local street gang. At any moment things could explode, and the trouble might come from Kamal, or from Rashid, or even from the Hamra street gangs.

Hadi also had Malek on his mind. He had awakened early that morning and had lain in the dark, his blankets pulled tight around him, and he had run everything back: the choices he had made and the things Malek had said to him. Hadi wasn't just handing boxes over; he was helping the drug deal happen. "That's wrong and you know it," he had said. And as Hadi thought back, he knew that no matter what he had told himself, he had known the first time Rashid had offered him ten thousand pounds that he had crossed a line. He had known in that moment that he had delivered drugs, and Malek was right: he had known it was wrong.

All the trouble his family was facing now had started with that decision. He was glad his mother wasn't suffering, and it had felt good to know his family had enough food. But it didn't make what he had done right. Every drug dealer could probably say that he was just earning money for his family.

And yet even after the disgust Malek had expressed and the argument the two of them had had, Malek had saved Hadi from Kamal, and what Hadi feared most was that Kamal had beaten Malek, might even have killed him. And if he had, that too was Hadi's fault. The problem was, he didn't know how to contact Malek, knew it was too dangerous to do so—dangerous for both of them. And he didn't know what he could do for Malek if he did find him.

All Hadi could think was that he had finally found a good friend, had promised to be friends forever, and then he had let his friend down. But when Hadi's life had been in danger, Malek had taken on Kamal and sacrificed his own safety. Now Hadi was hiding out, staying away, doing nothing to keep his promise. It was hard to imagine how he could do anything worse, and yet he had no idea what he could do to intercede for Malek.

The day seemed unusually long with such fears and thoughts running through Hadi's head. When he looked across the street, he could see how dejected Khaled was— no longer as frightened as before, but tired and sad. Hadi nodded to him now and then, and when the traffic let up, he would call to him, "You're doing a good job, Khaled!" Baba also came by a couple of times, and Hadi saw him talking to Khaled, probably encouraging him and no doubt telling him to keep stopping people, no matter how tired he was.

"When can we go home?" Khaled eventually yelled to Hadi.

"A little while yet," Hadi called back, but then, feeling sorry for his brother, "but not too long."

Finally, when the sun was angling low, Hadi walked across the street and asked Khaled how he had done. When they added up Khaled's coins, they found that he had taken in 5,750 pounds, but that included the 3,000 the nice woman had given him. Hadi had received more, but that counted the 10,000 the other young woman had given them. So the two together had done all right. The only trouble was, those two women had provided more than half their money, and Hadi and Khaled weren't likely to run into very many like them in the coming days.

When Baba arrived, he said that he had not done well at all. "I spent quite a while trying to find a source for items to sell," he said. "But when I asked people on the street where they got their sale items, some of them told me there were too many vendors on the street already. One man told me to stay away from him or he would report me."

"Who would he report you to?" Khaled asked. "The police?"

"No. There are men here who think they're in charge of everything." But he didn't explain beyond that. Maybe it was all he wanted Khaled to know, for now.

It was on the bus, on the way home, when Khaled had fallen asleep sitting in the middle but leaning against Hadi's shoulder, that Baba whispered to Hadi, "That man on the street told me I was pushing into territory where I don't belong. He said I was taking the chance of getting myself cut to pieces. Those were his words: 'cut to pieces.'"

"What about begging?" Hadi asked. "Do you think they care about that?"

"Probably. But if we stay off Hamra Street, I don't think they pay as much attention. The problem for me is, when I tried asking people for money, I got called more dirty names than I've ever heard before. I've got to find some-thing I can sell."

"I'm sorry," Hadi said.

"Sorry for what?"

The gloom he had felt all day darkened as he heard what Baba was dealing with. The sun was going down, and Hadi felt as though he was sinking, too, that he had dug a hole he and his family could never climb from. "Sorry that I got us into trouble," he said, "and we had to leave our corners."

"We can't think about that now. We just have to figure out how we can get by from now on."

Hadi looked out the window. The sea was blue and beautiful, and people were strolling on the sidewalk by the seawall. They were living their lives. Maybe some were on vacation and others were on their way home from work. All Hadi knew was that they looked satisfied. He wondered if any of them ever appreciated what they had, knew how badly he wanted to feel the way they did.

15

When Hadi, Baba, and Khaled arrived home, Hadi could see that Mama was upset. She was kneeling on the floor when they came in, but she stood immediately. "Rabia is sick," she said. "We have to do something." Rabia, wearing only underwear, was lying on a blanket. "She's been vomiting all day, and she has a fever—a high fever. I'm trying to keep her cool, but she's very hot. She needs a doctor. She needs medicine."

Hadi could see that Baba wasn't sure what to say. This was one more thing he hadn't needed. "Children get sick sometimes," he said. "We can't go to a doctor every time. She'll be better by tomorrow—or the next day."

"Come here. Touch her head," Mama said. "She's *very* sick."

Baba walked to her, knelt by Rabia, and touched the back of his hand to her forehead. Then he bowed his head, seemed to think things over. "We didn't come home with very much money tonight. Things didn't go as well as we hoped they would."

"Why did you try Hamra? Why change when you were doing so well?" Hadi heard frustration, even anger, in Mama's voice.

"I'm sorry. We hope to do better. But it's the right thing for now." He touched Rabia's head again. "I don't think she's in any danger," he said. "Let's see how she's doing in the morning."

Hadi heard his father's sorrow. His words sounded reasonable, but Hadi knew he would rather have sought help for Rabia. He was surely saying to himself, *My daughter needs to see a doctor and I can't help her*. But every day he had to measure what he had against the need for food. He didn't make decisions; his decisions were made for him.

Over the next two days, things got worse. Hadi and Khaled met no nice students who wanted to help them. They received coins, for the most part, and not nearly enough of them. Baba did even worse. Hadi took five thousand pounds from his shoe each day, and that made things seem a little better than they really were, but he knew at this rate his money would be gone before long, and now they had no fruit or vegetables from Garo.

Rabia was getting worse, not better. Hadi hoped the fever would soon be gone, but she wasn't herself. She merely lay on her blankets, her eyes looking distant.

"How are you feeling?" Baba asked her when they got home on the second night.

Rabia didn't answer for a time, but she finally said, "Sick."

"Did you eat anything today?"

It was Mama who answered. "She tried. But everything came back up. I'm worried what will happen if she can't start eating—or at least holding some water down. And she's burning up. Feel her."

Baba touched her head again, and Hadi saw his reaction. He shut his eyes, looked grieved. "She's worse," he said.

Hadi watched Baba's eyes go shut and knew he was trying to think what to do. "We don't have money for a doctor—or for medicine—but I'll go see the woman at the charity office and find out if she knows someone who can help us."

Mama said, "Take Rabia with you and—"

"Not yet. I don't want to carry her down there and find out there's no one willing do anything for us. But I'll hurry back. Just give me a few minutes."

When Baba stepped into the hallway and shut the door, the room was silent except for Rabia's heavy, ragged breathing. And by then Mama had begun to cry, just softly.

Baba returned in ten minutes or so, although it seemed much longer. He walked quickly to Rabia, at the same time saying, "The woman at the charity office told me about a hospital that doesn't turn sick people down—even refugees. It's not too far from Cola."

"But how can you get her there?"

Baba knelt by Rabia again. "I don't know. It's too far to carry her."

"Is there a bus that goes that way?" Mama asked.

"Yes, I think so. But I don't see how—"

"Baba," Hadi said, "I still have some money in my shoe. It's enough to pay for a taxi."

"Money in your shoe?" Mama asked. "What do you mean?"

Hadi didn't explain, nor did Baba. "We'll have to use your money," Baba said. "We can't take her on a bus." He didn't dress Rabia; he merely wrapped her in the blanket she was lying on, then picked her up.

"The blanket's too hot," Mama said.

"I know," Baba said. "I'll open it on the way." And then he looked at Hadi. "Run to the corner, find a taxi."

"All right," Hadi said. He hurried to the door and hopped down the stairs two at a time even in the dark. When he got to the street below, he turned and ran to a busier street to the north, where taxis often stopped on the corner. He spotted one, ran to it, and pulled open the back door. "My father is coming," he told the driver. "Wait for him."

"But have you any money?"

"Yes, I have money."

"Let me see it."

Hadi raised his foot and jerked his shoe off, then pulled his money out. He showed the taxi driver the folded bills.

But he didn't know the name of the hospital or how far away it was. "Just wait."

By then Baba was there. "Do you know the Makassed General Hospital?" he called out when he was still several steps away.

"Yes. Of course. But let me see how much money that is."

Hadi fanned out the bills. "Just get in, Hadi," Baba was saying, and he nudged Hadi toward the back door.

The driver nodded, mumbled that it was enough, and then he took off fast and wove through the traffic. Hadi didn't think he was hurrying because of Rabia, but only because that was how cabbies drove. All the same, Hadi was glad to be moving at a good pace. Rabia was moaning.

Baba opened the blanket to give her air, and then he touched her cheek. "We're getting you some help, little one," he told her.

It didn't take long—maybe fifteen minutes—to reach the hospital, even in the busy traffic. Baba told the driver to stop at the emergency entrance and he got out quickly, leaving Hadi to pay the fare. Hadi paid the man, even though the price seemed much too high: fifteen thousand pounds.

Hadi hurried inside, but what he saw was a throng of people filling up the waiting room, most of them standing because there were not enough chairs. "Hold her for a minute," Baba told Hadi. He handed Rabia to Hadi and then got in a line with four or five people in front of him.

Hadi held his sister, looked into her face. "It's all right," he told her. "You'll get some medicine. You'll feel better." He wasn't sure she was aware of the things going on around her, or whether she was awake enough to understand his words, but her eyes were now focused on Hadi's face, and what he saw in those eyes was desperation. She was a pretty little girl, but she looked pale now, the skin around her eyes yellow, her lips almost blue. Her breathing had turned into a gurgle.

Hadi stood with her twenty minutes or so before Baba made it to the front of the line, and then, it seemed, almost as long talking to the woman at the window. When he finally came back to Hadi, he said, "They'll look at her, maybe admit her if they have to, but they've run out of funding to treat her for free. I had some of my rent savings in my pocket, so I gave the woman ten thousand, but I had to promise to pay more later."

"How can you do that?"

"I don't know, Hadi. But her lungs sound terrible. We have to get help for her."

"What about medicine? Do we have to pay for that?"

"They'll give her what she needs, but they expect us to pay when we can. And I want to do that."

"We have to get some money. Somehow."

"I know. But let's worry about Rabia for now. We'll think about the rest later."

Baba took Rabia back from Hadi into his own arms, and he held her and talked to her. "I love you, little one," Hadi heard him say. "You'll be better soon."

But the words hurt Hadi. He was scared for his sister, but he also felt sorry for his father. Baba tried so hard, but nothing ever seemed to work out. The truth was, this illness, this expense, could put the whole family in the streets.

After a few minutes a nurse called out Baba's name, and he followed the sturdy little woman to a curtained area with a bed inside. As Hadi stepped inside the curtain, the nurse told him, "You can't be here. Sit down out there." She pointed to the waiting area Hadi had just come from. She didn't seem to realize that there were no seats. Hadi knew that she was way too busy, and probably tired, but he also noticed that she hadn't spoken to other patients with the same impatience.

So Hadi stood in the waiting room, and after a time Baba walked out and said, "A doctor finally came in and listened to her lungs, but I'm not sure what he's going to do. You might as well go out to the main lobby of the hospital and see if there's a place to sit down. I'll come out there when I know something." So Hadi wandered out to a hallway and walked around until he found the lobby. There were a few soft seats, and he was relieved to drop into one. He needed to rest, but more than anything, he needed to shut out all the worry.

He leaned back and stared across the room. He could hear two people—a young couple—talking, discussing the payments they would have to make. He tried not to listen.

Hadi didn't realize that he had fallen asleep until he heard someone speak his name. He opened his eyes, saw a face he knew, but didn't believe his own eyes for a moment. "Malek," he said. "What are you doing here?"

"Here's a better question. What are *you* doing here?"

"My little sister is sick. They told us this is the hospital that will take refugees."

"That's what the ambulance driver told me. That's why I'm here."

"What ambulance driver? What happened to you?"

A woman had been sitting in the big chair next to Hadi when he had first sat down, but she was gone now. Malek moved slowly to the empty chair and sat down carefully, not sliding back. His arm was in a sling, his head bandaged, and he was wearing hospital clothes: a bathrobe and slippers. "I've been here since the day Kamal beat up on you. Once you made it across the street, he didn't try to run after you. He came back for me. He didn't like that I helped you."

"What did he do to you?"

"He knocked me down, but I jumped up and ran from him. I tried to do the same thing you did—run across the street—but I wasn't so lucky as you were. I ran in front of a car, and I got hit."

Hadi gasped. "Hit by a car? Where are you hurt?"

"Almost everywhere. I broke my arm and some of my ribs. I'm bruised all over."

"What about your head?"

"It was cut open, and I had a concussion. I couldn't think straight for a few days."

"When are you going to go home?"

"Soon. The hospital doesn't like to keep people very long. I can walk around on my own now, so I think they'll kick me out tomorrow."

Hadi didn't like what he heard in Malek's voice. He was trying to sound light and easy about everything, but pain, and maybe disappointment, was in his eyes. It seemed to Hadi that the car had broken more than his bones.

"How did you know I was out here?" Hadi asked.

"I didn't. The nurse makes me walk, but I usually just stroll down the hallway. Tonight I decided to see what this hospital looks like. And then there you were. I didn't believe it at first. I had to walk up close to you and have a good look."

"Allah blessed us, Malek. I thought I would never see you again."

"Yes. I believe that." He looked more solemn than he ever had before. "I've wondered about you, Hadi. Did you have to go to a hospital?"

"No. Garo tied up the cut on my head and it healed pretty fast."

"What about your back—where he kicked you?"

"It hurts, but not too bad. You're a lot worse off than I am."

"I'll be all right."

But Hadi was seeing something in Malek's face. He had changed so much since he had first shown up on Hadi's corner. His cheeks were drawn in, and his eyes seemed darker against his pale skin. But the real change was that he hadn't smiled, not once.

"I'm sorry, Malek. You helped me get away, and then you paid for doing it."

"I couldn't let him keep kicking you, Hadi. I couldn't just stand there and let it happen."

"But I thought you hated me—because of the drugs."

"I didn't like that you did that," Malek said, and then he seemed to think for a time. "But it's what you thought you had to do. I understand that."

"It was wrong, though. You wouldn't have done it."

"We never know what we'll do until we're pushed to make a choice."

"I know. I've been thinking a lot about that. Last night I was trying to read my book. I read the part about crime and punishment. I don't think I understood everything it was saying, but the idea was that when one guy does something wrong, we all do. I think he means that the whole world gets worse when even one person does a bad thing."

Malek looked confused. "Do you believe that?"

"You said to me, 'That's wrong and you know it.' And that was true. I knew it was wrong and I did it anyway. People can't do that. The whole world turns into a mess if we do."

Malek was looking carefully into Hadi's eyes. "That's right," he finally said. "We can think of all kinds of reasons to do what's wrong, but that never makes it right."

"What's going to happen now, Malek?" Hadi asked. "Will Kamal come after you again?"

"No. My father talked to him, and he said I could come back to the corner when I'm ready—as long as I work hard. I never told Baba that Kamal was chasing me when I got hit, but Samir knows what happened. He came to visit me, here at the hospital. He told me that he warned Kamal that he better leave me alone from now on."

"I don't think Kamal is afraid of Samir. If he gets his chance, he'll come after both of us."

"Maybe. But my father told Kamal that he was sure you would never come back—because of Rashid—and that I won't cause him trouble again. Baba said that Kamal probably doesn't want to lose my brothers. They've been bringing in more money since the weather got better, and they don't cause him any trouble."

Hadi didn't know. Kamal could surely find other people to sell tissues, and he wouldn't forget that Malek had shoved him away from Hadi and let him get away.

Hadi glanced around the lobby. There were fewer people around now. Hadi wondered how much time had passed and how his sister was doing.

"Hadi," Malek said, "I don't think Kamal will come looking for you. As long as you stay away, he probably doesn't care what you do."

"What about Rashid?"

"That's different. Rashid won't want you out there,

knowing what you know and what you could report to the police."

"Maybe if I stay away and he doesn't hear anything about me, he'll figure that he scared me enough that I won't ever say anything."

"I hope that's right."

"But how can we ever see each other?" Hadi asked.

Malek didn't give a quick answer the way he always had before, but Hadi understood what he must be feeling. Once he got better, the only thing ahead for him was a return to the corner to sell tissues every day—all by himself.

"For now we have to avoid each other," Malek said.

"I know." It was all Hadi could do to keep his voice under control when he said, "You're still going to be an engineer. You're going to do it, no matter what."

Malek nodded, but not with his old firmness. "As far ahead as I can see right now, I have to keep selling tissues. There's no way I can go to school—at least, not for a long time."

"I know. But things don't always stay the same. Something good can happen to us, sooner or later. Are you still studying those engineering books?"

"Not since I got hurt. I'll try again when I get home. But they're hard, and my father loses patience with me."

"Just keep studying them—over and over, if you have to. That's what I do. I read a chapter, then I think about it awhile, and read it again. Some things start to make sense."

"Okay. You're a good example to me."

Hadi could hardly believe that. "You're the one who taught me," he said. "And we'll keep helping each other. I won't see you for a while, but we're friends. We'll always be friends. We'll keep our promises."

Malek nodded, but he didn't speak. Hadi could see that tears were filling his eyes. "I have to go," he said. "The nurses are going to be upset with me—for staying away from my room so long."

They both stood, and Hadi patted Malek softly on the shoulder. He looked too frail for anything more than that. But Malek did stop and look back after he had begun to walk away. "I hope your little sister will be all right," he said.

Hadi nodded.

"Hadi," Malek said, "when Kamal came back to the alley, he grabbed me and told me I had to tell him what intersection your father worked at. But I didn't tell him. That's why he knocked me down."

"That was brave, Malek."

The boys nodded to each other, and as Malek walked away Hadi could only think that he had to find Malek again, somehow, even if a long time passed before he could. But that thought brought him back to the present and all the things he was facing now. He needed to know how his sister was doing. He made his way down the hallway toward the emergency waiting room. He met his father halfway there, coming toward him.

"Is she all right?" Hadi asked.

"I came down to talk to you a while ago," Baba said, "but you were sleeping." He looked tired, worried. "She has pneumonia, Hadi. They've admitted her to the hospital, and they're giving her drugs that might help her, but she's very sick."

Hadi knew what Baba meant, but he refused to believe it. They were giving her medicine. She had to get better.

"We need to let your mother know what's happening."

"I'll take a taxi again, and—"

"No. We can't afford that. You'll have to walk, but I'll walk with you. I don't want you out in the street this late. It's almost ten o'clock."

"Don't you have to stay?"

"No. The doctor told me to go home. Rabia will be asleep all night, and there's nothing I can do now."

"But what if she . . . doesn't do all right?"

"I've thought about that. But Mama must be going crazy with worry by now, just wondering what's going on. And I can't change anything, no matter what happens."

"Rabia will be better in the morning. The medicine will make her better."

"Yes," Baba said, but then he added what Hadi expected. *"Inshallah."*

16

It was all Baba could do to convince Mama to stay home that night, and it was before daylight when Hadi heard Mama getting ready to leave. Baba came to Hadi, where he slept in the corner, knelt next to him, and said, "I'm going to walk with Mama to the hospital. I may walk back if Rabia is doing better. We'll take Jawdat with us, but you'll have to stay with your brothers and sisters."

"All right." Hadi hated the idea of staying in the room, not even going out to earn some money, but he was relieved to sleep a little longer now.

"Do you have any money left?" Baba asked.

"Yes."

"Look to see what food is here. Or buy a little, if you have to, but be sure the children get something to eat."

"What about tomorrow? If we don't work today, we won't have much left."

"I still have some of my savings for next month's rent.

We'll use it if we have to, and then . . . I don't know . . ."

Hadi didn't say anything, but he could see disaster coming. He lay on the cold floor, wrapped the blanket tighter around himself, and tried to shut out all his fears, but he couldn't think of any way to earn money, and he couldn't see how he and Baba, even with Khaled's help, could set aside enough for the next rent in the weeks they had left.

Gradually, a little light came into the room, and his siblings started to stir. So he got up and located some rice he could boil and half a package of flat bread. It was something, but the day might be long. He didn't know when Baba would return.

So Hadi offered the small helping of food to his brothers and sisters, heard some complaints, especially from Aliya. Still, he tried to keep everyone's mind off food by holding another class on the alphabet. But Khaled had little interest and Aliya was soon complaining that it was boring, so Hadi stopped. Before long, Aliya was teasing Samira, making her cry, and little Aram was crawling all over Hadi, wanting his attention. When Aliya and Samira started to quarrel, Hadi lost his temper. "That's enough," he shouted at them. "Your sister is *very* sick. Aren't you worried about her? Can't you be nice to each other for one day?"

But the girls only looked at him as though they had no idea what he was upset about. It was obvious they didn't understand how serious Rabia's illness was. He was immediately sorry he had raised his voice. He stood silent for a time, looked around at all his siblings, and then said, "All right. We all need a change. Let's go outside for a while. Get your coats on."

Aliya was especially joyous, but all the kids began searching about among the blankets for their coats. Hadi found his own coat in the corner where he always slept, and then he helped Aram zip up his coat and put on his little beanie hat, and they all walked downstairs.

Outside, the day was cool but clear, and they were all happy to be out of the room. The trouble was, there was little to do, only the crowded streets to walk through. So Hadi did something impulsive that he was almost sure he would regret when his money was gone. He took his brothers and sisters into a bakery and bought two manoushés, one with cheese and one with za'atar spice. Khaled was pleased, but the girls were joyous. They hopped up and down when they heard Hadi put in the order, and then, when they smelled the doughy crust as the manoushés came out of the oven, they both squealed with pleasure.

Hadi had the baker cut the round crusts into sections before he slid them into paper bags, and then they all walked outside and sat at a table out front. Aliya was upset when Hadi was slow in parceling out the sections, but when she took her first bite, she sighed and said, "Thank you, Hadi. Thank you. It's the best food I ever tasted."

Hadi knew she had eaten manoushés before, but they had been a rare treat. It hurt him to think how little good food she had tasted in her life. He found himself saying, "Someday we'll eat manoushés any time we want."

"When, Hadi?" she asked.

"Not so long from now, I think."

Hadi didn't believe his own words, but he didn't want her to lose trust that something better was ahead. And he wanted to find a way to give her those better days.

After everyone ate and then walked some more, Hadi took them back to the room. It was almost noon by then, and Hadi didn't want Baba to come home and find no one there. It was well into the afternoon before Baba arrived. And when he did, Hadi watched his face, fearful of what he would see. But Baba said, "Rabia is starting to get better. The medicine is beginning to take effect." Still, he looked relieved more than happy, and he came to Hadi and said, "You and Khaled should go back to Hamra and see if you can bring in a little money before the day is gone. Mama will stay with Rabia at the hospital overnight, so someone needs to be here with the children. But you two have more success than I do, and we'll need to feed them tonight. I'd like to do that without digging any more into our savings."

So Hadi and Khaled left immediately and rode the bus to the Corniche. Hadi worried that by the time they paid their bus fares, they would be lucky to come out ahead, but he was glad to get out of the house and try to earn something. Khaled was clearly not happy to go back to the street but surely hesitant to say so.

On the bus, Khaled said to Hadi, "I think we should sell roses like the kids on Hamra Street."

It was something Hadi and Khaled had seen: boys and girls going from car to car with roses for sale. Hadi had been impressed to see that their roses sold better than his gum ever had. "We can't do that," Hadi said. "They get their roses from the street gangs, and then the bosses come and take a lot of their money at the end of the day."

Khaled had been asking lots of questions about the gangs lately, and Hadi had gradually explained more about them, but Khaled said, "They probably still end up with more money than we do."

Hadi had wondered about that, but he and Baba had stayed away from the gangs all these years, and in their situation now, they especially didn't want to be noticed. But Khaled didn't know about Hadi's run-in with Kamal and about the danger he might face if Rashid ever found him. "I don't think Baba would want us to get involved with those people," Hadi told Khaled.

"We could ask the kids who sell roses. Maybe they just buy their own roses somewhere."

Hadi doubted that was true, but he was also tired of begging for money. So he decided Khaled was right, that it wouldn't hurt to ask. When they reached their usual street by the university, they continued up the hill to Hamra Street, and there they spotted two girls holding roses and waiting for the stream of cars to stop. "Do you mind if I ask you a question?" Hadi said to them.

The girls giggled. Hadi thought they were sisters; their smiles were just alike. One was slightly taller than the other, but they were both very thin. Still, they were dressed in clean clothes. They were too young to worry about covering their dark hair, so each wore a single, long braid down her back.

Neither girl answered him, but they didn't say no, so Hadi asked, "Would you mind telling me where you get the roses you sell?"

The taller girl shook her head, as though she wasn't going to answer, but then she said, "It doesn't matter. We just . . . get some each day."

Hadi knew what she was saying. Like Malek, she had been told not to answer questions about their source. "If I want to start selling roses," Hadi said, "is there someone I could talk to?"

"I don't know," the girl said, and she glanced at her sister, who only shook her head.

"I know about these things," Hadi said. "We're Syrians like you. We want to help our family. We only wondered—"

A harsh but whispered voice behind him said, "What do you want?"

The taller sister was quick to say, "He wants to sell roses. We didn't tell him anything."

Hadi turned around. He saw a man who was surprisingly like Kamal: young, dressed in a leather jacket, wearing a short, well-trimmed beard. And even in those few whispered words Hadi had heard that he was Lebanese, not Syrian.

"Why are you bothering these girls?" the man asked. It was an accusation more than a question.

"I only asked them about the roses. If my brother and I want to sell roses, how do we start?"

"You don't. There are already enough boys and girls doing that. We don't want any more on this street."

Hadi knew he had to be careful. "Okay," he said, "we just wondered."

"Stay away from these girls. Don't bother them again."

"All right."

Hadi was about to step away when the man said, "There are other things you might be able to sell. Have you ever sold anything on the street?"

"No," Hadi said.

But at the same time Khaled was saying, "Hadi sold gum, over in Bauchrieh. I've only—"

Hadi grasped Khaled's arm, held it tight, and Khaled seemed to understand that he had said too much.

The man took hold of Hadi's arm, but he looked at the girls. "The cars have stopped. Go to work," he said. And then he looked back at Hadi. He smiled, waited a moment. Lots of people were walking along the sidewalk, and Hadi had a feeling that the man was worried about attracting attention. He said, in a gentler voice, "So you've sold things before. And your name is Hadi?"

"Yes. My name is Hadi."

"Where do you live, Hadi?"

Hadi looked over at Khaled, told him with his eyes not to answer, and then he said, "Dekwaneh." He didn't know exactly where that was, but he had heard of a section of Beirut with that name, and it was the first answer that had come to him.

"You don't live in Cola?"

"No."

"And you've come all the way from Dekwaneh to bother two little girls?"

"We saw them selling roses, that's all. We wanted to ask them about it." He tried to smile, act natural. "We're sorry we said anything to them. We won't do it again."

"But your brother said you sold gum in Bauchrieh. Do you know a man named Rashid, who drives a taxi over there?"

Hadi felt a shock of fear run through him. He couldn't think what to say. He thought of running, but the man still had hold of his arm. He decided not to respond, but he knew the man had seen his body stiffen when he had mentioned Rashid.

"A man named Rashid is looking for a boy named Hadi, from Cola. He sold gum—and *other* things—in Bauchrieh. The word is on the streets by now, all over Beirut. That boy may not live long if Rashid tracks him down."

Hadi nodded, still didn't say anything. He glanced at Khaled, who was looking stunned. Hadi shook his head just enough to tell Khaled not to speak.

The man didn't say anything more for a time. He studied Hadi's face, and then he took a long look at Khaled. Finally he told Hadi, "We deal in roses here, and a few other things. We have our expectations, but we're not like Rashid. I'm sure you know what he sells. He's tied in with people who do *anything* to protect themselves. They kill without regret."

Hadi whispered, "I understand." But his voice was mostly gone. He felt as though he might collapse.

"I could hold both of you boys and turn you over to those people. But I don't want to do that." He looked at Khaled again and surely noticed how young he was. "But here's my advice: You need to get away from Beirut as soon as you can. Leave today if possible."

Hadi nodded. He was too out of breath to speak again.

"Go now. Your whole family should leave. Don't ever tell anyone we had this conversation, and don't show up in Hamra again. I won't be so lenient next time."

Hadi didn't bless the man, but he placed his hand over his heart and made a little bow. Then he and Khaled hurried down to the bus stop on the Corniche. All the way down the hill, and again on the bus, Khaled kept asking questions—about the man named Rashid, about leaving Beirut, about men who killed without regret. And Hadi kept saying, "I'll explain everything later."

When Hadi and Khaled stepped through the door at home, Hadi said to his father, "Come out to the hallway. We need to talk."

So Baba stepped into the hallway and Khaled tried to follow, but Hadi sent him back, and then he told his father what had happened and all the things the man had said to him.

It was dark in the stairway, and Hadi couldn't see his father very well. He watched his shadowed face and tried to judge his reaction. But Baba was silent. He asked no questions. When Hadi finished his story, he could hear Baba breathing, louder than before. He seemed to be pulling in all the air he could, maybe trying to calm himself.

"We can't leave with Rabia in the hospital."

"We don't have any money, either," Hadi said.

"I have the rent money. It isn't enough to last long, but it might get us out of Beirut."

"But where can we go? How can we buy food? How will we—"

"Hadi, I don't know. For now I'm trying to figure out how we can stay alive. Give me time to think."

Baba had been patient with Hadi through all these troubles, but he sounded as though he was trying to control his anger now. Maybe he was blaming Hadi for the mistakes he had made, or maybe himself. Or, Hadi thought, he was just outraged with everything: all that had happened since their home in Syria had been blown into rubble.

17

Baba decided that no matter how much danger they were in, the family couldn't leave Beirut until Rabia was well enough to travel. As it turned out, he was able to bring her home the next day—but mostly because the hospital didn't want to keep her any longer. A doctor was good enough to send her home with medicine—taken from his supply of free samples—so that was one expense they didn't have to worry about.

At the hospital, Baba had explained the whole situation to Mama, and Hadi was relieved that he hadn't had to look into her face and tell her that her life was turning upside down again—almost as bad as when they had been forced to leave Aleppo. She and Baba had to take Rabia in a taxi again, depleting their savings even further, but at least by the time they arrived, Mama seemed to have accepted the new reality. It was almost a blessing that she was still so worried about her little daughter. She said more than once,

"If Rabia can get better, and if we can all stay alive, I won't have anything to complain about."

When Hadi told her how sorry he was, she took him in her arms and said, "Hadi, your father told me that you delivered the boxes for the drug dealer because you wanted to help me get to a dentist. And don't forget, you did help me. I couldn't have lived with so much pain much longer."

She kissed him on the top of the head, and Hadi felt better. He was relieved to hear her words, but he knew at the same time that what he had told Malek was true. People couldn't do bad things even if they thought they had good reasons.

The hardest thing for Hadi was to explain everything to Khaled. He knew his brother looked up to him, and even though Khaled had heard the things the man in Hamra had said, he was clearly astounded when he heard Hadi admit that he had delivered drugs for a drug dealer. He said he understood, but Hadi sensed that he was disappointed his big brother would do such a thing. Baba had often spoken out against the evil that drug dealers caused.

Aliya and the younger children understood little of what was going on. But clearly they knew that their troubles had gotten worse. They had grown quiet and wary. Even Aliya seemed to know this was not a time to create problems.

Reality was hanging in the air, worse than the usual stink of their room. Baba let everyone know that no one could leave the building, and after he made a quick trip down the street to stock up on a few groceries, he stayed inside himself. He asked Hadi a couple of times about the exact words the man in Hamra had used. What Baba wondered was whether he could show up in a different part of Hamra and maybe earn a bit of money until Rabia was better, but Hadi repeated the warning that Rashid would kill the entire family. Baba thought he might actually go unnoticed in Hamra, but it was leaving the house that might be his undoing.

Rashid, somehow, knew that Hadi and his family lived in Cola, and he might have sent someone out to ask questions about a family named Saleh. Baba decided that the risk was too great. When they finally left the house, he told Hadi, they had to make a dash from the neighborhood. There was a big bus station at the Cola intersection, but Baba feared that it might be watched. He thought it might be better to take a bus from a closer stop, make their way to the Dora intersection, and then depart Beirut from there.

Three days went by and Rabia's lungs were clearing, but she was tired and weak. Each day Hadi wondered whether they might leave the next day. It was on the fourth day of hiding, in the afternoon, that Mama agreed Rabia could travel so long as she didn't have to walk very far. "It won't be far, and she can sleep on the bus," Baba told her. "But we have to go."

So Mama told the children to wear everything they could, under their coats. She carried Jawdat and Baba carried Rabia. Mama had tucked a bag of rice and some rolled-up bread into a grocery net, which she asked Khaled to carry.

Hadi grabbed his book, slipped it under his belt, and put on his jacket and then his coat over that, and then he waited, anxious. He carried Aram and walked down the stairs ahead of the others, and then he stopped at the landing at the bottom. Aliya and little Samira both looked terrified, their eyes wide. He wanted to tell them he was sorry, to make everything right somehow, but there was no way to do that. They had to escape—as fast as possible.

Hadi handed Aram to Khaled, and then he said, "Baba, let me look outside. I might recognize someone if we're being watched. Everyone wait inside until I come back."

He stepped out the door, prepared to scan the area. What he saw immediately was a man standing across the narrow little street by the electrical supply store. He had a dark hat on, pulled down close to his eyes. The man reacted when he saw Hadi, stood straight, and then walked forward and motioned for Hadi to come to him. By then Hadi had recognized the man; it was Fawzi. Hadi jumped back and then stepped into the apartment building. "A man is out there," he said. "One of Rashid's men." Hadi had thought about something like this happening; he already knew what he had to do. "Go out the back door. I'll make a run and lead him away from the house. I'll meet you at Dora as soon as I can get there."

"No, Hadi," Baba said. "He'll grab you and—"

But Hadi didn't listen to his father; he stepped back outside. He knew he could outrun Fawzi, if he could just get past him. But Fawzi was close now, standing in front of him.

"How did you find me, Fawzi?" He tried to laugh. He needed to stall for time so his family could get away, and he wanted to lull Fawzi into relaxing a bit.

Fawzi laughed. "We have you to thank for staying around and giving us time to track you down. Cola is a big area, but as we got closer, we found that people around here know your father, and they knew which building you live in. I didn't know your apartment number, but if you hadn't come out soon, I was going to knock on some doors. You just saved me the trouble. I'm afraid Allah let you down this time." He sounded satisfied with himself, almost friendly, as though he had won a little game of chess.

"What are you going to do to me?"

"That's not up to me. But I'm sure Rashid has some good ideas. Come on, let's go. Maybe we'll stop and get us a shawarma sandwich along the way. I'm hungry." And this he seemed to think was very funny. He laughed loudly and his voice echoed down the street, through the buildings.

At the same moment, another man—a younger man—stepped from the entranceway to another building. Hadi didn't know him, but he walked toward them.

"Let's go," Fawzi said, and he grabbed the shoulder of

Hadi's coat, but Hadi had not zipped it. He twisted and pulled his arms loose, and the coat came away in Fawzi's hand. Then Hadi sidestepped, avoided Fawzi's grab, and took off running—away from the other man. What flashed into Hadi's mind was that it was that young man who might have a chance to catch him, but Hadi could navigate the crazy alleys of Cola better than these men could. He might get caught, but he had to prolong the chase until his family was safely out of the neighborhood.

He ran hard and cut through traffic at the first corner, but when he glanced back, the young man had made his way through the cars and, if anything, was gaining on him. Then Hadi remembered the fence. He sprinted all out to an alley, turned in, and ran to the chain-link fence at the end. Kids in the neighborhood had dug out a little gap to use as a shortcut to another part of the neighborhood. He ran to the spot, threw himself down, and tried to scramble under. But his jacket caught on the metal points on the bottom of the fence. That delay was all the man needed. He grabbed Hadi's leg and began to pull him back. Hadi kicked wildly, broke the hold, drove himself forward, then kicked loose again when the man tried to grasp his ankle. He scrambled forward again, and he let the heavy wire tear his jacket, but in his haste to get up, it dug into his back. He felt the wire cut a long slice down the line of his spine.

He didn't think about the pain, didn't care. He jumped up, took a look back to see the man still down on his knees, cursing Hadi, and Fawzi now lumbering up the alley, trying to catch up.

Hadi ran along the fence and slipped between two buildings, out to another street, and then he ran through alleys, taking a varied route, one that he didn't think the men could ever guess to follow. He didn't know how they might try to find him, but he didn't dare run to the bus stop where his family was going. There was another bus route that headed toward Bauchrieh. From there he could make it through Bourj Hammoud to Dora. It was a long run to the bus stop, though—and eventually, a long walk, as Hadi wore down. He kept looking in all directions, looking for the men, for anyone who might be watching him. He spun all the way around a few times, surveying everything in sight.

When he reached the street where the bus stopped, an older woman asked him whether he was all right. She could see his torn jacket—and surely the blood. "I cut myself," he said. "It isn't too bad."

"It is bad. You need to get some help."

"I'll go to a hospital," Hadi said. "But I need to meet my mother and father. They'll take me there."

But then she did something that surprised Hadi. She was wearing a hijab and a long black robe, but she had a shawl over her shoulders—a pretty patterned one that looked expensive to Hadi. She took off the shawl and fit it inside his jacket and his ripped shirt. He felt the pain now, but he felt her gentleness, too. "When you get on the bus, press your back against the seat and against the shawl. That will slow the bleeding."

"I'll bring the shawl back to you if I can. How can I—"

"It's all right. You keep it. Give it to your mother. But you must get to a hospital as soon as possible."

"I will. I promise."

Hadi knew that the Makassed General Hospital was not far away, but if he went there, his family wouldn't know where he was. He had to get to them and then worry about the cut on his back. But it was hurting bad now, especially when he got on the bus and pressed against the seat.

The bus moved slowly in all the afternoon traffic, and Hadi's pain kept getting worse. By the time he reached the intersection by Bourj Hammoud, he knew he had a long walk to Dora—the same walk he had taken with a bloody head. And he realized what he had to do again. He couldn't walk all the way to Dora, look for his family, and then find some way to get help. He had to get to Garo.

Hadi was not as dazed as he had been the day Kamal had smashed his head against the wall, but he knew that blood was seeping through the shawl, through everything, down into the back of his pants. He tried not to look at anyone, so he wouldn't have to explain himself, and he walked hard. He was exhausted by the time he reached Garo's fruit stand. And when he stopped in front of his friend, Garo took a big breath. "What's happened to you now?" he asked. "Did that man beat you again?"

"No." But he was out of strength, out of breath, and for all he knew, out of blood. "I cut myself," he said. "On my back."

What followed was much the same as before. Garo took him to the back of his stand, helped him get his shirt off—the shirt Garo had bought for him. But once he cleaned Hadi a little, Garo said, "This is serious. I can't fix it. A doctor needs to stitch you up."

"I have to find my family. I told them I would meet them at the Dora intersection. They're in danger, Garo. Someone wants to hurt us—all of us."

"Why?"

"I've done things, Garo. I don't know how to tell you."

"It's okay. Don't try right now. But you can't walk there and back. You shouldn't walk any more at all. Wait just a minute." Garo went out front, and Hadi heard him letting down the canvas that covered his fruit stand. And then he heard nothing—except the street traffic—until Garo returned. "I have a taxi out front. I'm taking you to a hospital—the one on St. Joseph Street."

It was a hospital Hadi had seen many times when he walked through Bourj Hammoud, but it wasn't one that treated poor people. "I can't pay for a hospital," he told Garo.

"Don't worry about things like that right now. Let's get you over there."

"My parents won't know where I am."

"I know. We'll get you to a doctor, make sure they'll take

care of you, and then I'll take a taxi to Dora. You can tell me where to find them."

Hadi wasn't sure he knew where to find them, but he was having trouble thinking now. The pain in his back was filling his mind.

Just as Garo was helping Hadi into the taxi, a truck pulled up in front of the fruit stand. A man got out of the truck, but before he could say anything, Garo said, "Just stack the boxes in the back. I have to leave for a while."

"Leave?" the man asked. "Who's watching your stand?" Hadi heard his Syrian accent.

"No one," Garo said. "But people don't steal from me. They all know me in this neighborhood."

The deliveryman laughed. "That's how things ought to be," he said.

The taxi ride was short—but not fast. Traffic in Bourj Hammoud was packed tight. And then, in the emergency room, the woman at the desk had all sorts of questions about what had happened to Hadi and who was going to pay his bills. Hadi only said that he had been climbing under a chain-link fence and cut his back on the wire. Garo answered the other questions. He said that he would take care of the expenses.

"Garo, I'll pay you back. I promise."

"Don't worry about it, Hadi. We just need to get you fixed up."

The emergency room was crowded and people were

frustrated. They kept forcing their way to the desk to complain about their wait. The woman paid little attention to them, but she did get someone to put Hadi on a gurney and then wheel him to a curtained area—like the one the doctor had used for Rabia in the other hospital. A nurse cleaned the wound better than Garo had. But she was in a hurry, not as gentle as Garo, and not interested in talking to Hadi or doing anything but getting the job done.

"Will someone take care of him soon?" Garo asked her. "We've been here half an hour."

But that set off Hadi's other worry. "You have to go find my family," he told Garo.

"I know. But I won't leave until I know you're getting help. This cut is long and deep. It needs to be closed."

"I'll talk to the doctors. We'll do the best we can," the nurse said, and she walked away.

All the cleaning the nurse had done had fired Hadi's pain again. He clenched his teeth and tried not to cry. But as the pain subsided a little, he looked up to see Garo, who was standing at the head of the gurney. Hadi saw pain there, too, in those old brown eyes. "I'm sorry," Hadi told him. "I keep causing trouble for you."

"Oh, Hadi," Garo said, "it feels good to be useful. I've spent too much time alone these past few years."

"Thank you," Hadi said, and then he said something he had never said to anyone outside his family. "I love you, Garo."

Garo didn't say anything, but he patted Hadi's head, and Hadi saw tears in his eyes.

A doctor did appear soon after that, and he seemed motivated, more than anything, to take care of the matter quickly. He gave Hadi a series of shots, all down his back. Each shot felt like a knife stab. Hadi jerked every time and strained not to scream. But the doctor left then, and as the numbness set in, Hadi began to breathe normally. He finally had enough clarity to think about his family. He wondered whether they had avoided Fawzi and the other man and made it to Dora.

The doctor returned a few minutes later and began to stitch up Hadi's back, and at that point Garo said, "You should be all right now, Hadi, so tell me what your family looks like, and I'll go try to find them."

Hadi tried to think what he could say. "It's my mother and father and six children," he said, "the oldest is ten and the youngest just a baby. All of them are wearing winter coats—or maybe just holding them by now."

"All right. I'll go find them, and I'll bring them here."

Hadi thanked him again. But earlier Hadi had noticed something, and it had come back to his mind these last few minutes. Just as Garo was about to walk away, Hadi said, "Garo, that man who delivered the fruit to your stand, was he Syrian?"

"Yes."

"All right. I just wondered. But go ahead. Find my family."

So Garo left.

DEAN HUGHES

Once the doctor had sewn up the cut in Hadi's back and given him a tetanus shot—another sharp stab—he told Hadi that he needed to stay in the hospital overnight. He would need antibiotics to guard against infection, and he needed rest. So the doctor gave Hadi another injection to help with the pain, and even though Hadi tried, he couldn't stay awake after that.

18

Hadi was confused when he woke up. It took him a moment to remember that he was in a hospital, but the strange thing was that Malek was standing by his bed and he was saying, "Good morning, Hadi. How are you feeling?"

Hadi realized he must have slept all night. But how had Malek managed to find him? Hadi shut his eyes and tried to think, but he drifted back to sleep. When he opened his eyes again, it was Mama who was saying, "Hadi, wake up now. Tell us if you feel all right."

Hadi saw his mother, with Malek next to her, and strangely, Emil and Klara Riser. He couldn't imagine how they would know he was there.

"Hadi, does your back hurt?" Mama was asking.

He couldn't think whether it hurt or not, so he decided it didn't, but as soon as he said "No," he realized that he did feel something: mostly an ache, not a sharp pain.

"They don't want you to stay here—because we have no

money," Mama told him. "Your friend Garo said he would pay—but it has already cost him too much." She touched Hadi's forehead and then ran her fingers over his hair. "Do you think you can get up?" she asked him.

"Yes," Hadi said, but he didn't try. It wasn't the pain; it was his brain that seemed unready to take in all that was going on around him. He looked across the room at the Risers. They were smiling at him, and then Klara said, with her funny accent, "*Sabah alkhayr.*" "Good morning."

"Let me help you sit up," Mama said.

But Hadi asked, "Where's Baba?"

"Baba is with the other children. They're downstairs. They slept in the chairs in the lobby last night. I stayed here with you."

Hadi did sit up, with his mother's help, but now he felt more pain and he moaned. "The doctor said he would give you pills for the pain," she said. "Do you need one now?"

"No." The pain was not terrible, and mostly, he needed to be awake. He looked at Malek. "How did you get here?" he asked.

"I was released from the other hospital a few days ago, and I'm supposed to rest for a while longer—but I was nervous, doing nothing, and I kept wondering what had happened to you. I was afraid Rashid might have found you."

"Do you think he's still looking for me?"

"I think so. He sent Kamal to ask me where you lived. I told him I didn't know, but my father didn't realize what was going on, and he told Kamal you lived in Cola. So Rashid knew where to look. I wanted to warn you, but I didn't know how. You had told me about Garo and where he had his fruit stand, and I wondered if he would know anything about you, so this morning I walked over to see him, and he told me you were here in the hospital."

"What about you?" he asked the Risers. "How did you know I was here?"

It was Malek who answered. "When I was walking down St. Joseph Street to the hospital, they drove by and spotted me. They stopped to find out how I was doing. All they knew was that the two of us weren't at the corner anymore. I told them what I could explain, partly in Arabic and partly in the little French I know, and they didn't understand everything, but they finally got the idea that you were in a hospital. I think they could see that I wasn't holding up very well, so they offered me a ride."

Klara Riser had listened to all this and seemed to have understood most of it. She asked Hadi in her version of Arabic, "How are you feeling now? We have . . ." But she couldn't come up with the word she wanted. She looked at Malek and spoke to him in French for a time.

Malek said to Hadi, "I'm not sure I understood all that, but she said they have worried about you. She said, 'We like you and Hadi. Emil and I call you *our boys.*'"

Hadi nodded to her. "*Merci,*" he said. "I'm doing all right," he told her in Arabic, and she nodded her understanding.

"They're from Switzerland—the French-speaking part," Malek said. Hadi had known they were from Switzerland, but he didn't know there were different parts to the country. He was amazed to think that the Risers cared about him enough to visit him here in the hospital.

"Hadi," Malek said, "no one knows how you hurt your back. Did someone cut you?"

"No. I crawled under a fence, and the wire caught me and ripped my back open. But people were chasing me—Rashid's men. Fawzi and another guy."

"Will they be checking hospitals to find you?"

Hadi wasn't sure about that. He still felt only half-awake. But he said, "They chased me in Cola. And this is far from there. They know I cut my back, but I don't think they knew how bad it was."

But now everything was becoming clear: Hadi had run away, escaped for a time, but he was still in danger. So was his family. Rashid was probably still looking for him.

A nurse had come into the room. "So, you're awake," she said, and she smiled at him. "How are you feeling?"

She seemed very young, and her voice had some life in it. That was a sound Hadi hadn't heard at the other hospital. "I'm not too bad," he said.

"Does your back hurt?"

"Yes. But I don't want medicine. It makes me sleep."

She laughed. "I understand. We won't give you anything so strong as you had last night."

Mrs. Riser asked the nurse whether she spoke French, and the nurse said she did. Then Mrs. Riser said something in French, and the nurse turned back to Hadi and said in Arabic, "She wants to know if you plan to go home now."

Hadi shook his head. He wasn't sure what he dared to say to the nurse, or to the Risers. He only said, "No. We can't go back to our building."

Emil Riser spoke, and the nurse translated: "Are people still trying to hurt you?"

"Maybe," Hadi said. But then he admitted, "They might hurt my whole family."

Emil had understood. "But why?" he asked in Arabic.

Hadi hesitated, but then he said, "They sell drugs. They're afraid I will be a witness against them."

The Risers looked to the nurse, and she did translate the words, but she seemed concerned. Mama said, "Don't say anything else, Hadi. You must be careful."

Hadi knew that Mama was right.

But Klara was asking something else, and the nurse translated: "We talked to you one day about going to school. Is it something you still would like to do?"

"Yes. Of course," Hadi said. "But not now. There are too many . . . problems." The Risers glanced at each other and seemed confused, but Hadi had decided he better not explain too much, especially to the nurse.

The nurse took his temperature, and then she listened to his heart and lungs. She told him he could stay at the hospital until a doctor came by to check on him one more time. "I'm sorry you can't stay longer," she said. "You need more rest."

She left, and Mama helped Hadi lie back on the bed. He was wide-awake now, and scared. His family could still take a bus, maybe, and get to some other city, but the bus fare would use up their money. Where would they sleep that night? How would they buy enough food? Hadi could see in his mother's eyes that she was worried too.

The Risers were talking to each other. They weren't just chatting. Hadi didn't understand the words, but he could tell that they were discussing something serious. Malek told Hadi, "I only understand part of what they're saying, but I think they're trying to figure out some way to help you."

Hadi had no idea what that could mean, but it made him think of Malek's problems. "Malek, what is your family doing to earn enough money now?" he asked. "You can't go back to the streets yet. You're still in pain. I can see that."

"I do have some pain. In my ribs mostly. But I have to work. We're almost out of food."

"But you can't sell tissues all day. Not yet. And you shouldn't have come here. It was too far for you to walk."

"But I needed to know that you were going to be all right. Garo told me that your cut was bad. He was worried about you."

"I'm not hurt as bad as you, Malek. And I'm worried what might happen to you now."

"Maybe people will feel sorry for me, with my arm in a sling, and buy more of my tissues." Malek tried to smile, and he stepped closer and put his hand on the bed by Hadi's pillow. He took a long look at Hadi. "I don't know what's going to happen to either one of us," he finally said.

Malek was losing hope, and Hadi couldn't think of a single thing he could say to change that. What he knew was that boys like him, and like Malek, had a better chance of ending up in garbage dumpsters than working in good jobs and living in nice houses. So he only said, "I'll help you if I can. I promise."

"Okay. I promise too . . . you know, if I can find a way. My father is doing a little better lately. His hand is healing, and I heard him tell Mother that he'll start looking for work again. Maybe he means it this time. If things go better for us, I'll find a way to get help to you." Malek touched Hadi on the shoulder. And then he said, "I need to leave. Don't try to contact me for a while. Rashid will be asking me what I know about you, but I'll never tell him where you are. I'll check with Garo sometimes. If you can, let him know how you're doing, and he can tell me."

"All right. And if things go better for us somehow . . ." But he couldn't finish his sentence. He saw no way for that to happen. Hadi also wanted to say that he hoped he would see Malek again, but he was afraid he was feeling too much, that he couldn't get the words out.

Malek ducked his head. Hadi knew that he was

embarrassed. "Goodbye. For now" was all he managed to say.

"Let me drive you home in my car," Emil said in rather clear Arabic.

Malek seemed to know he needed the help. He nodded his agreement.

"Go downstairs. Rest. We must talk to Hadi a few minutes."

Malek nodded again, glanced one more time at Hadi, and then walked from the room. There was silence after that, and Hadi knew that his mother and the Risers were giving him some time.

But it wasn't long before the door opened and Garo stuck his head in. "May I come in for a moment?" he asked.

"Yes, yes," Hadi said. "I'm awake now."

Garo came in and greeted Hadi's mother. Clearly the two had gotten acquainted.

"Did you find my family yesterday?" Hadi asked. "Is that how they got here?"

"Yes, of course. It was not difficult to recognize them."

"He brought us here in a taxi," Mama said. "All of us crowded in." And she said to Garo, "Thank you for helping us." Then she told Garo about the Risers and how kind they had been to Hadi.

Garo, as it turned out, spoke some French, and he talked with the Risers for a time. Hadi had no idea what they were saying, but again he sensed that this was a discussion, not a mere exchange of greetings.

After a time, Garo turned to Hadi and said, "Yesterday,

you asked me whether the truck driver who stopped at my fruit stand was Syrian. Why did you ask me about that?"

Hadi tried to remember. All of that now seemed a week ago. "I was surprised that a Syrian had a job like that. I wondered if my father could get work of that kind."

"Just as I thought," Garo said. "In the taxi, on the way to find your family, I tried to think why you would ask, and that's what I decided you were thinking. What I hadn't known was that your father was a truck driver in Syria, but on the way here to the hospital, I asked him, and he said he had done that kind of work all his life. So I then asked him, if something was available with the company that delivers my produce, would he be interested, and of course, he said he would."

"But how can Syrians get work like that?"

"I wondered about that too. I had my doubts, but I called the manager of the trucking company, and he said that the government allows Syrians to do farmwork, and delivering fruits and vegetables can be called farmwork. Then he said that he could use another driver or two. He might be willing to hire your father, but he would need to talk to him first. It doesn't pay an awful lot. It would not be every day, either, but it might work into that. I talked to your father downstairs, and he seemed very pleased. He's going to contact the manager."

But Mama said, "We have to leave Beirut. Those men are still looking for us. How could he—"

"I just talked to these nice people from Switzerland. They have some ideas. They work for a charity organization. They think they might be able to find a place for you to live—maybe in Jounieh, if that's not too close to Beirut."

Hadi had heard of Jounieh. It was north, not very far, but still out of the city. He didn't know whether that would be far enough to move, and he didn't know if he would still need to sell gum, or if the job driving a truck—if Baba could get it—would give them enough money to live on. He was afraid to believe that these things could all work out, but it was something to hope for, and he hadn't felt such lightness in his chest in a very long time.

"If we moved to Jounieh, could my husband drive the truck for the company you spoke of?" Mama asked.

"Yes. He would deliver to many places, but he would start out each morning in Dbayeh. That's not too far from Jounieh. He could take a bus to the headquarters and pick up his truck there each day."

Hadi wondered. Would he have to deliver in Beirut? How dangerous would that be? But he decided, for now, not to doubt. He would let himself hope, even if only a little.

"These nice people want to take you to the office of their organization. They don't know whether they can work anything out for you, but they want to try."

Hadi looked at the Risers. He was astounded. *"Merci"* was the only thing he could think to say.

Mama went to them, kissed them on their cheeks, and cried.

"Garo, thank you," Hadi said.

"I'm glad if I can help you, Hadi. Maybe you can go back to Syria someday, but until then, you deserve something better than what you have faced here so far."

"Thank you," Mama was saying. "*Allah yebarkak.*"

"And may Jesus Christ bless you, my friends," Garo said.

"*Inshallah,*" Hadi said to himself, and he thought he finally understood why his father used the word. So much was beyond Hadi's—or anyone's—control.

19

Mr. Riser drove Malek home, and then he returned. When Hadi was released from the hospital, the Risers took Hadi and his mother, along with Aram and Jawdat, in their little car, and they hired a taxi to take Baba and the rest of the family. They drove to Jounieh, north of Beirut. It was a busy city between the sea and the mountains, with a crowded highway running through it. But the office for the nongovernmental organization that the Risers worked with was on a quiet street, and everything inside was new and clean.

The office, however, was only one section of the building—a few rooms—on the main floor, and it was not fancy. Emil and Klara took everyone into a waiting room with couches and chairs and asked the family to sit down, and then they talked to a woman at a desk. She invited the two of them to enter an office, and they didn't return for quite some time. Hadi was nervous. He wanted something good to come of this, but he had gotten used to disappointments.

Hadi was amazed when the woman at the desk asked if everyone would like some water. "Yes, I would," Aliya said, and the others were all nodding. So the woman left the room through another door, and when she returned she was carrying a box full of water bottles. The children were polite in accepting them, but Hadi could see the confusion in their eyes, as if they had no idea why someone would give away something so wonderful.

The Risers finally returned. "Please come in," Klara said, and she gestured for Hadi and his mother and father to enter the office.

Mama carried Jawdat with her, but Baba asked Khaled to look after the other children. Khaled clearly didn't like the idea, but he didn't argue.

Hadi, with his parents, entered a smaller room with a desk and some chairs. A woman behind the desk spoke to them in Arabic. "Come in," she said. "Take a seat. My name is Mona." But then she said something to the Risers in French.

Mona, who sounded Lebanese, was wearing a yellow blouse, and her fingernails were bright red. She reminded Hadi of some of the women he had seen in the cars he approached on the street. Her hair was gray, cut very short. To Hadi, she looked like a rich lady, but she seemed tired and didn't smile; he wondered whether she would be as helpful as the Risers had been.

She looked at Baba. "Emil and Klara tell me that you were bombed out of your home in Aleppo. Is that right?" she asked.

"Yes. We've been in Beirut for almost four years."

"But you have no papers?"

"No. At first we had a permit that admitted us as 'temporarily displaced people.' We renewed the permit after a year, but then the government raised the renewal price very high—far beyond what we could afford. They told us to go back to Syria if we couldn't renew, but there's no way we could do that. Most of Aleppo is destroyed, and the war has not really ended. We could go to another city, but there is no work in Syria now."

"They tell me that you may have found a job here, that you might be able to start driving a truck for a company in Dbayeh. Is that right?"

"Yes. *Inshallah*. It's only a possibility for now, but I'm hopeful that I will soon start working."

"But without a residency permit, I'm sure you know that's illegal."

"Our friend Garo tells us that it's considered an agricultural job—because I would deliver fruits and vegetables. Most of the drivers for this company are Syrians."

"Strictly speaking, it's still illegal, since you didn't apply for a renewal of your papers." She leaned forward and looked at a sheet of paper on her desk. "But as you say, some managers are only too happy to let Syrians work—so long as they don't have to pay them as much as they would pay Lebanese employees."

Baba nodded, but he didn't say anything.

Mona was still looking at the notes in front of her. Hadi thought maybe it was her own writing—maybe things she had jotted down when talking to the Risers. But now she leaned back and removed her eyeglasses, held them in her hand. She seemed to think for a time. "People in Switzerland—and other places—donate money to our organization. They tell us to help refugees. But they also tell us to follow the laws of the land. They have no idea how complicated that is. The Lebanese government has never accepted the international standards for treatment of refugees. I want very much to help you, but I have to be careful not to break laws. Added to that, our budget shrinks each year, and I have limited money to work with, so everything becomes harder."

Hadi was sitting up straight to avoid touching his back to the chair. He was feeling more pain now, and a kind of numbness was buzzing through his head. Still, he waited anxiously for Mona's conclusion, but she didn't offer one. The room fell silent, the only sound the restless movements of Jawdat, sitting on his mother's lap. Hadi was almost certain that nothing good would come of this. He felt himself sink into his chair. Nothing ever seemed to change.

Mona set her glasses on the desk, and then she looked at Hadi. "What happened to you? How were you injured?" she asked.

"I cut my back trying to climb under a fence," he said.

"And why were you trying to crawl under this fence?"

Hadi could see where this was going; all chance for help would soon be lost. "There are men in Beirut who control the people who sell things on the streets," he said. "If you don't do everything they say, they beat up on you. That's happened to me before." That was true, of course, but Hadi couldn't look her in the eye. He knew he wasn't really answering her question.

"So you did something they didn't like?"

"Yes." But Hadi felt his chest tighten. She was looking at him with doubt in her eyes, as though she knew there had to be something more to this. So instead, he said what he wanted her to know. "I want to go to school more than anything. I'm learning how to read, but I need to learn mathematics—and everything. I want to have work someday, and—"

"But that's just the problem. We can possibly help you go to school, but I can't let you think that will solve all your problems. You can't become a citizen of Lebanon, so you can't take a job other than farmwork, as your father said, or construction. People here believe there are far too many Syrians refugees and that you're a burden that is destroying the economy. The Jordanians feel the same way. The European countries opened their doors for a time, but now they say they have done enough for you. America has stopped taking Syrians, and Canada and Australia are taking only a few. So here we are, trying to change minds, trying to help refugees, but no one is willing to offer you a way to live once you do finish school." She folded her arms and sat stiff for a time, but then she added, "It breaks my heart to tell you such things, but those of us who want to help are dealing with an almost impossible situation."

"We know these things," Baba said. "We understand. But for now we need to eat, and we need to have a place to live."

Hadi couldn't stand to hear all this. "If I go to school," he said, "maybe things will be different by then. I want to own a shop. Garo, my Armenian friend, was a refugee, and his father started a business. I want to do something like that."

"But everything has changed, Hadi. The doors that were open to Armenians, long ago, are closed now."

The room was silent again.

That seemed the end of everything. Mona was telling him that she couldn't help.

But Hadi didn't want to accept that. "Do you know a book by a man named Kahlil Gibran? It's called *The Prophet*."

Mona smiled. "Everyone in Lebanon knows this book," she said.

"Kahlil Gibran said, 'Even those who limp, go not backward.' I've thought a lot about that lately. I just keep telling myself, I have to go to school, and then maybe something will change. If I stop walking forward, then I know nothing good will happen."

Mona set her glasses down, leaned forward, stared at Hadi. "You've read *The Prophet*?" she finally asked.

"Most of it."

"But I thought you hadn't gone to school."

"I haven't for a long time. But I've been trying to improve my reading."

"By reading Gibran?"

"It's the only book I have."

Mona shook her head slowly back and forth. "Hadi, you astound me," she said. And then she looked toward the Risers and talked with them for a time in French. When Mona finally looked back at Hadi, she said, "Klara believes that we should help you go to school. And I must say that any boy who wants to learn as much as you do deserves a chance. But I'm concerned about something. I still want to know why those men were chasing you. You never really answered my question."

Hadi was actually relieved that she hadn't believed his half-truth. He was tired of being ashamed of himself. "I delivered drugs," he said. "I didn't sell them, but I gave them to people who came by to pick them up. I did it because my mother was in pain and needed to see a dentist. But I knew it was wrong, and I tried to quit. The men who were chasing me were drug dealers, and they were afraid that I would testify against them in court."

Mona was nodding, looking solemn. "I understand how these things happen. These drug dealers know how to draw you boys into their system. It's awful. I'm not blaming you, but you have to understand, my donors would be outraged if they knew I was using their money to help a drug dealer. And I'm afraid that's how many of them would see it."

Hadi tried to think what he could do. "If you can't help me go to school, can you at least help my family find a place to live? I'm the one who did something wrong, but I've put them in danger too."

Klara said something, and then Mona spoke with the Risers again. Maybe she was telling them that she couldn't help Hadi and his family, and maybe the Risers were arguing with her. They seemed agitated.

After a time, Mona said, "Emil and Klara have been telling me what a good boy you are, how hard you have worked for your family. And they say that the drug dealers took advantage of you. They think I should not mention the drugs in my report and that I should enroll you in a school. What do you think of that?"

"If you can't do that, I understand."

"What would Kahlil Gibran say about that?"

Hadi tried to think what he would say. "I don't know exactly," he said. "But he said, 'Love has no other desire but to fulfill itself.' I've thought about that for a long time, and I've talked to Baba about it."

"And what do you think it means?"

"We should love people . . . but not for any reason."

Mona smiled. "So you want me to love you and give you a chance?"

"I didn't mean that. I just mean that the world gets worse

when we do what's wrong, and it gets better when we care about each other. I did something I shouldn't have done, and now I have to hope that the world can forgive me."

"So you want me to forgive you?"

"Yes. But maybe the people who give you money could forgive me too. I can limp forward, but I would like to walk."

"Oh, Hadi, you're a philosopher." She was nodding her head, maybe thinking.

"He studies his book every night," Mama said.

"That's impressive," Mona said. And then her voice changed, as though she had reached a decision. "Our organization has a program for children who are too old for first grade but haven't had a chance to go to school. If I enroll you, I'm sure you will advance quickly. And then, perhaps, we can enter you into an afternoon session in a Lebanese school."

"That would be wonderful," Baba said. "Could our other children—"

"Yes. I could include all those old enough to go to school."

But Mama had a question. "Is the school here in Jounieh?"

"Yes."

"Where could we live?"

"We have some housing. It's only temporary, but you can live there for a time, without paying rent, until you can manage on your own. There's something we recognize. Displaced people—refugees—can manage all right if they get a start, but as Hadi said, it's the world that has to reach out to them and lift them to the first step on the ladder."

Hadi looked at Mama, who had begun to cry. Baba's head was down. Maybe he was trying not to cry, or maybe he was ashamed that he had to accept such help. Hadi didn't know. He only knew that relief was spreading through him, relaxing his muscles, letting him breathe again in a way he hadn't for a long time. It seemed as though he and his family might finally see better days.

But then another concern hit him. "I have a friend," he said. "He worked with me on the street. He got beat up—and he got hit by a car. And it happened because he tried to protect me. His father has no work. Is there something you can do for his family?"

Mona let out her breath, seemed to sag a little. "There are thousands of families like that in Beirut," she said. "I can't help them all. The truth is, I don't really have room in my budget for you and your family. It's only because Emil and Klara brought you here and spoke so strongly for you that I've decided to make some adjustments and do what I can for you. I simply can't take any more right now. I'm sorry."

"But Malek deserves help. Is there another office like this one that he could go to?"

"I don't know. Every nongovernmental organization is facing the same problems that I am. People around the world felt sorry for all the displaced families at the beginning of the Syrian war. But most people forget after a while. There are so many problems in so many places, they get tired of hearing all the sad stories." She turned then and asked the Risers a question, listened to them, and then she told Hadi, "Klara tells me that they know some people in another organization who might help—and they know this boy you're talking about. They will try to see what they can do."

Hadi nodded. "Malek wants to be an engineer," he said. "He's smart, and he can read everything. He helped me improve my reading while we were selling things on the street together, and we're friends now. We promised to help each other."

"That's fine. You've spoken up for him. That's all you can do for now. Leave it to Emil and Klara to see what they can find out."

But Hadi could tell that she still didn't understand entirely. "If I can own a shop someday—or do something like that—and he becomes an engineer, we want to help other people. People like us. We promised we would never forget each other, and we would figure out how we can help other people who are displaced—the way you do. We don't want kids to beg or—"

"Hadi, it's hard for you to comprehend what it would take to get all the children off the streets of Beirut, not to mention the rest of the world. There's no way to solve all the problems we face."

"But Malek and I want to do what we can."

Mona smiled, but only sadly. "It sounds good to say that. But you've only seen a tiny part of the overall problem.

There are sixty, maybe seventy million displaced people in the world. People across the world feel bad about that, but not many care enough to do something significant to help."

"But that's why we can't stop trying."

Mona smiled again. "I wish you luck, Hadi. But the challenges are bigger than you can imagine. If I can help you today, I'll feel good about it, but when I take the bus back to my house at night, I'll see children on the street and I'll know I've hardly touched the problem."

"But you don't stop trying," Mama said. "Hadi shouldn't stop either."

Hadi was surprised, but very pleased that Mama would speak up for him. He had the feeling that she was coming back to life.

"Yes," Mona said. "Hadi should keep trying. I'm sorry that I've sounded so negative." She smiled at Hadi. "Maybe your generation can do better than ours has done. I hope so. I really do."

20

After the meeting with Mona, the Risers filled their car twice and drove Hadi and his family to a building not far away. The apartment they would live in, at least for a time, was better than Hadi had imagined. It had a living room, a kitchen, and two bedrooms. And there was a bathroom with a shower that they didn't have to share with other people. There was even furniture: actual beds in the bedrooms and a couch and soft chairs in the living room. But more than anything, the place looked clean, smelled clean. There were no water stains on the walls, no mold, not even any cockroaches running around on the floors.

The kitchen cabinets were stocked with pots and pans and dishes. The bedroom closets were filled with sheets and blankets, and the bathroom cabinet with towels. Mama looked happier than Hadi remembered her since they had made their way to Lebanon, and Baba seemed more himself. He sounded determined when he said, "We won't be here long. I want to earn enough on my job—if I get it—to rent our own apartment. Then someone without a job can move in here."

What amazed Hadi was that he seemed to trust that something was going to work out. The next day he met with the manager of the trucking company, and two days after that he went to work. When he came home after his first day, Hadi heard him tell Mama, "The company is getting into its busy time of the year. My boss said he can use me almost every day. I'll make much more than I ever did on the streets."

"*Alhamdou Li'Allah,*" Mama said, giving thanks.

"Yes," Baba said. "*Alhamdou Li'Allah.*"

Hadi thought he still ought to help in some way, but Baba said, in addition to a better income, he could bring home plenty of fruits and vegetables that were too ripe, like the produce Hadi had brought home from Garo's fruit stand. "I won't be paid the way I was back in Syria, when I was making long hauls all the time," he told Hadi, "but we won't worry about having enough to eat. Mama can start cooking some of the good things you ate when you were little."

"If we need to save up to get our own apartment, I could sell gum here in Jounieh—you know, after school."

"No. I don't want you and Khaled to go out into the street ever again. I'm sorry you ever had to do that."

Hadi was relieved—and thankful—but he still had one great fear. "Do you think Rashid is still looking for me?" he asked.

"I don't know. If he knows we've left Cola, maybe he'll decide we're gone for good and he'll stop searching for you. I doubt he would look for you all the way out here. And the manager told me he would put me on a northern route, away from Beirut."

Hadi hoped he and his family really were safe, but he hated to think of Malek's life by comparison. Malek was probably working the corner by himself now, still injured and still having to satisfy Kamal. And Malek's family surely didn't have enough money to live a decent life. Hadi kept trying to think what he could do for them.

Over the next couple of weeks Hadi felt a change in himself that he hardly understood. He had started school and it was even better than he had imagined. Khaled and Aliya also attended school, and they were still learning to read, but Hadi was now beyond that and far ahead of most of the children in the class, so the teacher, a Lebanese woman named Miss Saad, let him read on his own much of the time, and he read everything she gave him. He wanted to understand more about science and about the world—the countries and all the sorts of people who lived in other places. Everything was interesting to him now. He had felt for a long time that he knew too little, but now he realized how much there actually was to know and what a tiny fraction of it he had even been aware of.

Miss Saad was teaching him addition and subtraction,

and he began to learn multiplication and division. He took problems home with him every day, and Miss Saad said he was learning math faster than any student she had ever taught. "You're very smart, Hadi. Do you know that?" she asked him one day.

"A friend of mine told me I was smart," Hadi told her. "But I wasn't sure."

All that was pleasing to Hadi, exciting, but he didn't tell anyone the other side of what was happening to him: he still woke up at night sometimes, sweating and breathing hard. And he saw the scenes in his mind: the sound and flash of explosions, the man who was dying from breathing chlorine gas, and Marwa in her mother's arms, the sound her mother made as she moaned and cried. As he lay there, he always managed his fear the same way: He thought of the bright-pink blossoms on the flower tree, and he tried to imagine that it was still alive, reaching into the soil for sustenance, not giving up. He knew he had to be like that. Allah had blessed him, and good people were helping him; now he had to make the most of whatever opportunities came to him.

Khaled didn't love school as much as Hadi did, but he liked to play soccer during recess, and the sorrow that Hadi had seen in his eyes when the two had worked the streets together was gone. He was a boy again, and Hadi thought that was what he needed to be.

Aliya, finally freed from that dark room where they had lived, was almost too exuberant. Mama had to calm her down sometimes, but she was behaving much better, being nicer to her sisters and especially to Mama. Hadi heard Mama tell Baba how pleased she was to see all the children so much happier than they had been during those dark days in Cola.

One Sunday, about a month after the Salehs had moved into their new apartment, the doorbell rang, and when Hadi opened the door, there was Malek standing in front of him, grinning. It was like that first day Hadi had met him at the corner.

Behind Malek were Emil and Klara Riser, smiling too. "I wanted to see you," Malek said, "so the Risers brought me."

"Come in," Hadi said. "Come in." He had never kissed Malek on the cheek before. But it felt right now, so Hadi kissed him on both cheeks, as Syrians normally did.

Malek looked around. "This is a nice place," he said. Then he greeted Mama and the children. Baba was not yet home from work.

The Risers did their best to talk to Mama, but Hadi asked Malek, "Are you still working on the corner in Bauchrieh?"

"Yes, I'm back there," he said. He shrugged. "But it's not too bad now. Like you always said, people buy more tissues when the weather is better. And some days I sell gum. It's good not to sell the same thing every day."

Hadi didn't know what to say. It was painful to think of Malek still having to work at the old corner.

But Malek was quick to tell him, "Emil and Klara have

been talking to people. Maybe—someday—they can find work for my father. They won't stop trying."

The Risers told Malek—and Malek told Hadi—that they had things to do and would be gone for an hour or so. Malek could stay and talk to Hadi. Hadi and Malek walked outside so they could talk by themselves. There was a parking lot behind the apartment building, with a low wall around it. The two sat down on it. To Hadi, it seemed the same as before, when they had sat next to each other and eaten shawarma sandwiches behind the wall. But there was no rain. The season of rain was almost over.

They talked about the corner and about Malek's latest idea about how to approach people in the cars. "Lately, if their windows are open, I've been saying, 'I hope you're having a nice day.' I wait a second to see if they look at me. Then I say, 'I also hope you can make *my* day better.'"

"Do they like that?"

"Not really. But I like to say it. Sometimes it surprises people, and they at least look at me."

Hadi laughed, but then he asked, "Do you think Rashid is still looking for me? Has he asked you where I am?"

"Rashid is gone. Samir told me that he's in jail. He said the police are cracking down more than before, trying to get drug dealers off the streets. But Samir knows about Rashid sending his men to chase after you, and he's angry about that. He's hoping, this time, they can come up with enough evidence to keep Rashid locked up."

Hadi felt another moment of relief. But Malek said, "Samir also said that as soon as the police put a few dealers in prison, others will show up. As long as people want to buy drugs, someone will supply them. I guess that's right, but he told me not to get involved with any of the taxi drivers—so I stay on my corner and I don't cross the street."

"That's *my* corner. I told you that a long time ago." Both boys laughed. Hadi was reminded again that he could joke about it now, but Malek was there every day still listening to drivers insult him. "So how is your family doing?" Hadi asked. "Are you managing all right?"

"Well . . . not really. Emil and Klara have gotten a little help for us—some food and clothing. And sometimes I walk over to see Garo and he sells me fruits and vegetables cheap, the way he always did for you. But I don't know about rent this next month. My father has been . . . I don't know, upset. He put a lot of hope in finding work, and it just hasn't happened so far. My brothers and I are bringing in more than we did in the winter, but with Kamal taking a lot of what we earn, it's just not enough to live on."

The boys were silent for a time, but then Malek smiled. "At least I'm still handsome."

"Yes," Hadi said. "And smart. Almost as smart as I am."

"Oh, so now that you're in school, you think you're smarter than me."

"I certainly do. Miss Saad tells me every day how fast I learn."

"But if she saw me, she would fall in love with me. She couldn't help it."

"She's about forty years old. So I don't think so."

"That doesn't matter. All women fall in love with me."

"I guess I'm lucky," Hadi said. "Girls don't pay any attention to me."

"Actually, you look good. It seems like you've grown, and it's only been a month or so since I saw you last."

"I'm eating better food," Hadi said. "And Mama said I'm standing up straighter. I guess that might be right." But Hadi knew he had to do more than joke with Malek. He needed to encourage him. "I'll tell you the truth, Malek," he said. "You're still the smartest guy I know. And you're going to do great things in your life. I still know you will."

Malek nodded a couple of times. "I keep telling myself that," he said. "I hope it will happen."

But he didn't sound confident, and that worried Hadi. "I thought nothing would ever change for me," Hadi said, "and you kept telling me not to think that way. I really believe things will change for you, too. You have to believe that."

"I know. I'm trying." He raised his head higher, and Hadi could see that he didn't want to let himself give up. "I'm still reading those engineering books, and at least my father's been willing to help me understand them. He says I'll do well if . . . or when I get a chance to go to a university."

"That's right. And I hope we can get together once in a

while now. I keep reading my book, but I still don't understand most of it. You always made more sense of it. It would be great to read some chapters together and then talk about the ideas."

"So what are you thinking now?" Malek asked. "Do you still want to have a shop of your own?"

"A bookstore, and I want to read every book before I sell it." He laughed. "But how can we do it, Malek? How can you become an engineer, and how can I open a bookstore? Mona, the woman who helped us get this apartment, told me that we can never get jobs in Lebanon—not good jobs—even if we go to school."

"I don't know. I still think things will change. The war in Syria has to end someday, and engineers will be needed to help rebuild everything. And people will read books again."

"It's nice to think that will happen," Hadi said.

Malek was wearing a shirt with a picture of a bottle of Pepsi-Cola on the front—no doubt something given him by a charity organization. He crossed his arms over that picture now, and he shut his eyes. "We have to keep hoping, that's all," he said. "And do everything we can for ourselves. We can't always depend on other people to make things better for us."

That sounded right to Hadi, but it was Garo and the Risers—and Mona—who had pulled his family out of the trap they had been caught in. "Let's remember what we've talked about," Hadi said. "Let's help each other, and then, if we become what we want to be, we'll help other people—people like us."

"Sure. It would be good if we could do that."

"I know we can't solve all the problems in the world, but if we helped a few people, and they helped a few, that's at least moving things in the right direction."

Malek was nodding. "Sure. That's right."

"I need to help you stay in your apartment. That's what you need right now."

"But that's not something you can do, Hadi. You can't worry about it."

"I'm going to do something. I'm just trying to figure out what it is."

Malek was looking down again, and Hadi thought he knew what he was thinking—that Hadi was only talking, that there was really nothing he could actually do. "I'm just glad things are going better for you now, Hadi. Maybe, before long, things will get better for me, too."

But this struck Hadi hard. It was like the two of them had been drowning together, and someone had pulled Hadi out of the water and left Malek behind, about to go under. Hadi had to pull Malek up now. Somehow. So Hadi said, "We promised, Malek. I'll think of something."

After Malek left that afternoon, Hadi couldn't stop thinking about their conversation. Malek was laughing again by the time he left, and Hadi had laughed with him, but all evening a picture kept coming back to Hadi's mind: Malek sitting with his head down, his voice more than his words admitting that he was discouraged.

Hadi kept asking himself what he could do, and mostly he thought about the Risers and how they might be able to find help from a charity organization. But that could take months—or might not ever happen. Hadi needed to do something—do something himself. He had known for a while what it might be, but it seemed far too little to help very much, and it was the last thing he wanted to do. It was not until he was sitting in school the next day, enjoying a book—and thinking again of Malek back on the corner— that he knew he had to do it. Maybe others could help more, but Hadi had to do what he knew how to do.

After school, Hadi walked to a little market down the street from where he lived. He had seen Chiclets for sale there and had laughed to think of what they had once meant to him. But today he asked the manager if he could get a discount if he bought a whole carton of them. He bargained a little, and he got a good price. He still had a bit of money left over from the cash he had hidden away in his shoe before he had left Beirut, and it didn't seem likely his family would need it now. He bought the carton, walked to a bus stop, and rode a bus into the busy part of Jounieh. When he spotted a "flower tree" thickly laden with pink blossoms, he thought it was a sign, and he got off the bus at the next corner.

Hadi stood at the corner and waited for the cars to stop

at the streetlight. Then he walked to the driver's side of the first car. He showed the driver his boxes of Chiclets. The driver wouldn't look at him, so Hadi walked to the next car, and the next, and then on up the line. No one bought his gum at first, but he kept trying for a couple of hours, and he earned a little money. His plan was to work every afternoon and into the evening and save all he could before the end of the month. And then he would find a way to get the money to Malek.

He would keep his promise, the same as he knew Malek would. It felt to him as though he had found at least a small way to give of himself.

AUTHOR'S NOTE

My wife, Kathy, and I lived in Beirut for a year and a half, from 2016 to late 2017. As part of a humanitarian effort, we taught free English classes. The majority of our students were refugees from Syria or Iraq. While many think of refugees as living in camps, only a small percentage of refugees in Lebanon are housed in the tent cities often used in other countries. The majority receive minimal help from nongovernmental organizations and primarily rely on whatever jobs they can find—usually low-paying menial work—or on such makeshift enterprises as selling trinkets on the streets.

Not far from our apartment, at a major intersection, we saw one such boy on the corner selling Chiclets virtually every day, no matter the weather. We wondered what his story was, but he couldn't speak English and we couldn't speak Arabic. We bought gum from the boy every time he approached our car, and he always thanked us and blessed us. We began to wonder about his life, whether he went to school and whether he had a family.

Eventually, through a translator, I was able to interview the boy (I won't use his name), who was thirteen at the time, but he said he had started selling on the street when he was eleven. We knew by then that many of these street children were younger than he was. I learned, by talking to the boy, the outline of his history, but this book is not his story. It's my imagination of such a life, based on what he told me and what I learned through research. Most refugees in Beirut, like this boy, are people who lost everything to the wars in their nations but who are amazingly resilient. It was from them we learned the word "*inshallah*." It was also their resilience that became my inspiration to write *Displaced*.

Lebanon is a beautiful little Mediterranean country, full of wonderful people. They never stopped surprising us with their hospitality. It's next to impossible to enter a Lebanese home without being fed. And what excellent food it is! One of my fears is that readers of *Displaced* will come away with the wrong impression of the many welcoming, loving people we met in Beirut.

And yet Lebanon is a complicated place, with a great mixture of people from different cultures, religions, and ethnic backgrounds. The country has outlasted its own fifteen-year civil war and has worked to rebuild itself. More recently, since the Syrian war began, Lebanon has accepted approximately a million and a half Syrian refugees into their tiny country, and that influx has become almost overwhelming. About a third of the people living in Lebanon have fled from other countries, and while NGOs, churches, and charity organizations from all over the world have tried to help, budgets of all these organizations have tightened, and emigration for Syrians to other lands has been mostly closed off. Poverty among the refugees is clearly evident, and it's painful to see. At the same time, Lebanese feel the loss of a once thriving economy that inspired the name "Beirut, the Paris of the Middle East." It's not surprising that some of the Lebanese people resent the influx of refugees, but it's also no wonder that those refugees feel helpless in the face of their reality.

We observed some local people venting their frustration on the children who approached their cars. But most did not. Still, a few insults a day to children caught in such a difficult situation is surely heartbreaking. And this is the reality I hoped to convey in the stories of my fictional characters: Hadi and Malek.

As Americans, Kathy and I always knew that we were understanding the complexities of the Middle East in only a superficial way. But we know what we experienced in our English classes: Lebanese, Syrians, Iraqis—people of many faith traditions—all sitting down together, laughing and talking and enjoying one another. We met in our classes skilled craftsmen, laborers, dentists, professors, teachers, engineers, university students, computer specialists—people of every background. But as refugees, they had no opportunity to work in their chosen careers. They had been waiting months, and often years, to receive the chance to emigrate, but only a few nations have left their doors open—slightly— and the options for Syrians have almost disappeared.

All our students were trying to improve their circumstances. We learned, as we have experienced before in many places: Governments may contend, but people can almost always find common ground and understanding. We were always moved by the gratefulness our students expressed in spite of their circumstances.

Those who found their way to our classes had often brought some savings with them to Lebanon, or they had obtained some sort of menial work. They could find the time, mostly in the evenings, to take our classes. But the poor who have immigrated to Lebanon often live in slums, or in makeshift hovels, and they try to survive in circumstances too overwhelming to overcome on their own. We came away feeling that the world simply must not forget them.

At the beginning of this book, I quoted Patrick Kearon. He is an international leader in the Church of Jesus Christ of Latter-day Saints, the organization that asked us to offer humanitarian help in Lebanon. Let me remind you of his words again, but in a larger context:

Being a refugee may be a defining moment in the lives of those who are refugees, but being a refugee does not define *them*. Like countless thousands before them, this will be a period—we hope a short period—in their lives. Some of them will go on to be Nobel laureates, public servants, physicians, scientists, musicians, artists, religious leaders, and contributors in other fields. Indeed, many of them *were* these things before they lost everything. This moment does not define them, but our response will help define us.

Patrick Kearon also spoke at a meeting of faith leaders at a European Union summit in Brussels in 2016. He said:

We have learned that, for our own people, their attitudes toward refugees have been determined by the way they have reached out to them. When you interact with and help somebody, you grow to love them, and that is what has happened.

That is also what happened to us. The circumstances for many refugees are far too dire for anyone to expect them to find a path back to solvency entirely on their own. What we learned, however, is that when we offered a bit of help, their resilience and faith blossomed. They began to hope. The worst thing we can do is to fear them as "the other" and turn our backs on them.

Kathy and I think often of the boy on the street we

watched for eighteen months, and we wonder what is happening to him now as the refugee crisis grows only worse. Surely he deserves a chance at an education and a path to a better life.

I wrote the book, but Kathy has collaborated with me at every stage of its progress, and I thank her for her support as well as her unguarded critiques and corrections. I also appreciate the help and guidance I have received from my editor at Atheneum, Alexa Pastor, who has lovingly but not always tenderly advised me toward better writing and a better book. And finally, thanks to authenticity reader Serene Dardari, who helped me with my Arabic and some of the details about Beirut.